Also by Alcyoné Sumila Starr

YOU ARE THE ULTIMATE MAGICIAN-
Fearlessly create the life of your dreams

You Are the Ultimate Magician

Know Thy Power and Be Free

BOOK 2

ALCYONÉ SUMILA STARR

BALBOA.
PRESS
A DIVISION OF HAY HOUSE

Balboa Press books may be ordered through booksellers or by contacting:

Balboa Press
A Division of Hay House
1663 Liberty Drive
Bloomington, IN 47403
www.balboapress.com
1 (877) 407-4847

Print information available on the last page.

ISBN: 978-1-9822-2015-0 (sc)
ISBN: 978-1-9822-2021-1 (e)

Balboa Press rev. date: 01/23/2019

ACKNOWLEDGEMENT

I acknowledge and thank my unseen friend, Gladiator, for giving me the spiritual truths and the experiences there of, which I have shared in these books-

YOU ARE THE ULTIMATE MAGICIAN-Fearlessly create the life of your dreams.

YOU ARE THE ULTIMATE MAGICIAN-Know thy power and be free. (Book 2)

Without Gladiator's benevolent and loving presence in my life I could not have written these books.

DEDICATION

I dedicate this book to Tom for his belief in me that I could write the book, and to Leshma for her enthusiasm and constant encouragement to me to write and publish the book.

INTRODUCTION

(Why I wrote this book)

Life was happening to me (as I thought at the time), as it happens to most of us. It was average with family, friends, children and a job that gave me opportunity to travel the world. My friends thought I was lucky to have everything in my life, alas, I felt differently. I had kind of a sub-conscious belief that something vital was missing from my life. I did not know what it was, and so, could not put a name to it. On the whole, it made me restless and dissatisfied. One day a colleague of mine suggested I should read the book 'Autobiography of a yogi' by Paramahansa Yogananda. Well, I did and thus started my journey on the so called spiritual path. I began seeking in earnest, with all my passion to find the missing ingredient of my life. Of course, there was the problem – I didn't know precisely what I was seeking and so, I didn't know what to focus on. I tried everything that I could lay my hands on. I read hundreds of books on spirituality, self-empowerment, body-mind-soul, Bhagwat Gita to name a few. I attended work-shops, seminars and webinars without getting any clarity. I continued my search. I learned meditation, Mantra, Astrology, Astronomy, Tarot, past-life regression therapy, N.L.P., hypnotherapy, E.F.T., Quantum mechanics, Angel therapy, the list goes on- you name it and I did it, but to no avail. But I stuck to my seeking.

After decades of research and spiritual practices, my tenacity paid. I started getting answers and insights that I found difficult to believe at first. But, when experiences followed my insights, I learned my first lesson, which was, I need not seek anything outside of me. I realized I am the source of all that I perceived. I am creating circumstances in my life to physically experience my desire. The whole process is so simple but so difficult for most, including me, once upon a time, to understand and believe. But, once I got it, it changed me from within. My life transformed in un-believable ways.

The only reason why it took me decades to understand it, to really get it, is that I was not aware of what I was seeking. I certainly do not want you, or anybody else, to struggle for years, like I did for want of clarity. I believe it is a birth right of every human to know who or what he/she truly is. So, this book, in the form of a spiritual fiction, came into existence for the sole purpose of acquainting every reader with the basic universal law that empowers beyond measure and brings transformation way-beyond expectation. This book is in simple language with step-by-step instructions that every reader can understand, easily assimilate and incorporate in daily life, with outstanding results. Here, I would like to add that all information and instructions, given in the book by the character called 'Gladiator', have actually been passed on or channeled (for want of a better word) from a non-physical intelligence by the name of Gladiator.

So, are you ready for an extra-ordinary life? If so, I encourage you to read this book, and easily create the life of your dreams.

That is why you are here my friends!

THE STORY SO FAR

The story so far, from the first book of the trilogy of "YOU ARE THE ULTIMATE MAGICIAN-Fearlessly create the life of your dreams"-

Mark, who had followed Julie into the library, said "Alaska, do come. It is something quite different. I know you will like Gladiator's talk on spirituality. I believe it is very empowering."

"No Mark. I am not wasting my time on these woo-woo things. The name 'Gladiator' itself irritates me. Does he look like a Roman Gladiator? Forget it Mark. I am not coming." Said Alaska, a student at the university, and settled down to read her book. But, alas, after her friends left, she could not focus her attention on the book in her hands. Accepting defeat to her curiosity, she searched for 'Gladiator' on the web. When she was scrolling down his website Alaska was startled to find herself looking into a pair of Indigo blue eyes of a man in a photo at the bottom of the page. Alaska gasped when she felt the man smile at her. She felt a peculiar sense of urgency to meet the guy.

Gladiator's favorite statements were- You are the ultimate magician; You are the creator of your reality; You can fulfill your desires just by desiring them; You are powerful beyond the comprehension of your mind; Anything is possible if your believe it, and Dream, then follow your Dream and then, live the life of your dreams. Alaska wanted to verify these bold statements.

Gladiator encouraged people to learn who or what they truly were, and to unlearn the old limiting beliefs about themselves.

To know the truth behind Gladiator's teachings, Alaska joined all his on-line courses. She learned to meditate and did spiritual practices taught at his spiritual schools. She attended Gladiator's holographic presentation and seminars.

Alaska soon realized the authenticity of his work and finally became convinced that her thoughts, beliefs and feelings were shaping her current life, as Gladiator said. Anything she wished for and felt unbridled enthusiasm for, always came to pass. She was 100% responsible for the way her life turned out to be, but of course, no one believed it.

Now, it became her passion to help Gladiator spread the spiritual knowledge to the far corners of Earth.

Alaska's friends said "Gladiator's sheer presence is enough to start an avalanche of change in us. He disrupts our mediocre life and catapults us into a dream world, a world we thought was not possible."

After a seminar, Alaska would invariably ask Gladiator "When do I see you again?" and he would ask "When do you want to see me?" and her involuntary answer would be "soon". The next moment he was gone, but Alaska would hear "Your wish is my command, Princess".

Alaska would wonder if she was hallucinating, or if Gladiator did say that, and if he did, why did he say that?

CHAPTER 1

The young woman looked tired and defeated as she entered the arrival hall of the airport. She looked at her six years old son, who was small for his age, tightly holding her hands dragging himself to the nearest chair. Both his legs were encased in iron braces. She had stopped going out altogether as she found it very difficult to carry her son with heavy braces. Today she had brought him to the airport because her husband was coming back after more than a year of absence. She felt happy and excited but when she looked at her son, her joy evaporated and she started her silent chant "Help my son, help my son, Gladiator, if you have any power, help my son."

Exactly 21 days ago, when she was randomly searching for new healing modalities for her son, she had come across a picture of a man with Indigo eyes piercingly looking at her. She couldn't look away from the picture. Involuntarily she had said "Heal my son, please heal my son" and then doubt crept in and she had asked "Can you?" She was stunned to see the man in the picture smile at her, and at that moment she knew for sure this man could heal her son. She found out that the man was called Gladiator. He had spiritual schools and taught about spirituality besides being a rich business man.

Today the woman was feeling very disheartened by the daily struggle of looking after her disabled son. She resumed her silent chant "Help my son, Gladiator, help my son". When she thought she saw a tall man with Indigo eyes walking towards her, she jumped up and dragged her son saying "Johnny, Gladiator has come! The ultimate magician has come. He will heal you."

Little Johnny stumbled behind his mother and somehow reached the man, who appeared too tall to him. He looked up at the man and asked "Are you Gladiator, the magician?"

The man replied "Yes."

The boy persisted and asked again "The ultimate magician who can heal?"

The man replied with a smile "Yes, I am the ultimate magician but so are you young man!"

The boy sadly said "No, I am not."

The man said "Yes, you are. Do you want a proof?"

The boy nodded his head.

The man said "OK. Tell me what you want."

The boy thought for a second and excitedly said "A little birdie in my hand!"

The man said "Alright, stretch your arm, like so, and close your eyes."

The boy closed his eyes and waited with his arm stretched out in front. The man looked at a little bird which had somehow got inside the arrival hall. In the next moment the little bird swooped down and perched on the boy's arm chirruping loudly. The boy opened his eyes shouting "I am a magician, I am a magician, look Mom, I made this birdie come to me!"

The woman closed her eyes and fervently prayed "Gladiator, heal my son, heal my son", and the next moment she was astounded to see her son running after the little bird screaming "My birdie is flying away. I have to catch it!"

The woman turned towards the man, but he was not there. She frantically looked around, but he was nowhere to be seen.

She fell to her knees laughing and crying and saying "Thank you, thank you, thank you, Gladiator, thank you, thank you, thank you................"

CHAPTER 2

Alaska looked at her watch as she entered the towering building of De Winter enterprises. It was 2.55 PM. She thought again she should have accepted Maxim's offer to pick her up instead of opting to come here on her own. She didn't want to be late for her first appointment with Maxim De Winter, owner of the De Winter Enterprises, and well known for his spiritual work as "Gladiator" around the globe.

She quickly entered the building and was thoroughly impressed by the gleaming spacious lobby. It looked more like the lobby of a 7 star hotel than that of a corporate office. She saw a row of elevators on the right side of the lobby but remembered Maxim telling her not to take those elevators but to walk straight through the lobby and take the elevator which will be on her left side. She was walking fast across the lobby when she was stopped by a young man in suit and tie. He asked her politely "May I help you?"

Alaska replied "I want to meet Mr. De Winter."

The man said "I don't think Mr. De Winter is in, but I will call and check for you. Please come this way." Saying this, the man led Alaska back in the lobby to his desk.

Just then Alaska heard "That won't be necessary George. I am in, as you can see." Alaska spun around and was thrilled to see Maxim walking towards her. She gave him a big smile and said "I think I am late. Sorry."

"Hmm, I don't think you are late. It is exactly 3." said Maxim, with a smile while guiding her to the elevator.

Alaska asked him "How come you were here at the exact time?"

They entered the elevator. As the door closed Maxim replied "The moment you entered the building I sensed you had come. I realized that the security system of this place will make you go through the routine checks before letting you come up, and that would mean, the end of our coffee time before the seminar. So, I came down to ensure we can have coffee before leaving for the Miller High school for the seminar."

Alaska murmured "Thank you."

She could feel the silent and fast ascension of the elevator. Alaska guessed it must be moving very fast daring Earth's gravity to slow it down. The thought made her smile.

Maxim said with a twinkle in his Indigo eyes "Yes, you are right Princess."

Elevator stopped and the doors opened. Maxim guided Alaska to the impressive door to his domain. He, as usual, moved so quickly that Alaska could hardly appreciate the paintings on the walls but she did observe the massive flower arrangement in the center of the hall, right under the dazzling chandelier. She silently said "Wow!"

Maxim was holding the door open for Alaska to enter. As she walked in, she heard Maxim say "Dorothy, coffee please."

Alaska thought "Dorothy? Who was Dorothy and anyway, where was she? She hadn't seen anyone in the spacious lobby."

Just then Maxim added "What about something to eat? May be some cookies for my little friend?"

"Coming up Mr. De Winter!" Alaska heard the reply through the half open door.

As soon as Maxim closed the door Alaska complained "Why did you ask for cookies? You make me sound like a little girl who is always hungry."

"Aren't you Princess?" Maxim said with a quizzical look in his Indigo eyes. He continued "Anyway, relax. Dorothy and her assistants are here to supposedly make my life easier and so, they are happy to do so."

There was a knock at the door. Maxim said "Come in."

Alaska saw a man walk in with a tray.

Maxim said "Ah, thank you, Benito. Is it your very own special brew? This lady here is very fond of coffee. Let us see if she approves of your special brew."

"I hope, Madam will like it." saying this he placed the tray on the coffee table and silently withdrew from the room. As if on cue, a lady, smartly dressed, entered the room with a crystal tray piled up with cookies.

"So, this must be Dorothy" guessed Alaska.

Dorothy looked at Alaska with a smile and said "Hope you like the cookies. These are from a special bakery down the road."

Before Alaska could thank Dorothy, Maxim summarily dismissed her by saying "Thank you, Dorothy. That will be all."

As the door closed after Dorothy left, Alaska loudly exhaled and relaxed. She had been so busy watching the interaction between Maxim and Dorothy and Benito that she had not looked at the room where she was still standing. Now she turned and looked and again silently said "WOW!" She went to the wall that was all glass, to look at the panoramic view of the city. "What a view!" she thought "Everything is perfect, beautiful, rich and opulent."

Alaska was startled to hear a soft buzz from Maxim's huge table. Maxim talked with someone and before he finished his talk, someone else walked-in in the room. Maxim asked with a smile "Brent, can't it wait till tomorrow?"

The man looked at Alaska in surprise and said "Yes, of course, Mr. De Winter" and quickly withdrew from the room.

Maxim turned to look at Alaska who was still standing near the glass wall, but before he could say a word there was a buzz again and Maxim said "Can't it wait?" After listening for a moment he said "Alright, put him through." He spoke for quite some time over the phone. Alaska was surprised to note that Maxim spoke in fluent

French. No end to his accomplishments, thought Alaska. Every passing moment, made her feel more out of place.

As Maxim finished speaking, there was again a buzz. Maxim laughed and said "Brent, no more" but he listened to what was being said on the phone.

Then he said "Send him in."

By now Alaska was feeling overwhelmed and wanted to run back to her Dorm.

The door opened and a tall man entered the room carrying some papers in his hands.

Maxim said "No, no time to look at the documents but I want you to meet my friend Alaska."

He looked at Alaska and said "Princess, meet my friend and my right hand man, Brian."

Brian must be Maxim's age. He looked intelligent and good natured but right now he was staring at Alaska in stunned silence, as if he could hardly believe what he saw.

Brian recovered quickly and said with a smile "Nice to meet you Alaska. I have heard so much about you from Mr. De Winter."

He looked at Maxim and said "I will leave these documents here." Saying this he went out, closing the door softly behind him, before Alaska could respond.

She stood silently expecting to hear the telephone buzz or to see someone walk in again. She was feeling absolutely out of place. This was not her world. She felt unnerved. Alaska looked at Maxim, who was gently smiling at her in his usual way. Today he looked what he truly was – a billionaire entrepreneur with business holdings around the world. This was his world and there could never be any place for her in this powerful business empire. She felt sad and disheartened.

Alaska was silent for a moment, and then she said "I always thought of you as Gladiator, the brilliant spiritual teacher, but today, seeing you here in this place, it hit me that you are beyond my reach. We cannot be friends. I cannot fit in here, in your rich world."

Maxim softly asked "Does it matter?"

Alaska kept quiet. She was feeling overwhelmed. She wanted to go home. Maxim came and stood very near Alaska. He took both her hands in his and asked again "Does it really matter?"

Alaska mumbled "I don't know. You are holding my hands and staring at me like that, I can hardly think!"

Maxim smiled and said "You mean I have to either let go of your hands or stop looking at you before you can answer? But I thought my vibration did not affect you now. You yourself are now vibrating at a high frequency".

When Alaska didn't say anything, Maxim said "Your wish is my command Princess". Saying this he let go of her hands but remained standing near her, waiting for her answer.

Alaska looked up expecting to see annoyance but Maxim's Indigo eyes had the same gentle, indulgent look as always.

Alaska involuntarily closed her eyes to think what was bothering her, why was she reacting the way she was when she heard Maxim say "I thought it was I and only I that mattered to you Princess. I, the formless, I, the eternal being, that you befriended beyond time and space, do not change just because I am not meditating with you on board a yacht or speaking at a seminar. The 'I' remains the same everywhere. Don't let the forms confuse you. Forms come and go because they are transient, I am not!"

After pausing for a moment he said "Open your eyes, Princess and look at me."

Alaska opened her eyes and looked into Maxim's Indigo eyes in total awe. She felt, she was in a different dimension altogether. She could hear Maxim but could not see his physical form instead she saw a brilliant column of light. She heard Maxim say "Can you see the real 'I' that I am?"

At that moment Alaska came to the present with a jerk. She nodded her head.

Maxim smiled and gently said "I am just like the coffee you like. The coffee does not change whether it is served in a china cup or a mug or a glass, in a restaurant or at home. Coffee remains the same.

I am your coffee Princess. I remain the same whether on board a yacht or at a seminar or in this office."

After a short pause he asked "Do I taste different here?"

"What?" asked Alaska.

With a smile Maxim repeated "Do I taste different here, in this room?"

Alaska couldn't stop giggling and asked "How can I taste you Maxim?"

"Princess, that means, without tasting me, the coffee, you passed your judgement that I am not good enough to be your friend or good enough to work with, based only on the outer trappings! Oh, how heartless can you be?" teased Maxim.

Alaska tried to explain "Maxim, here you appear so important, so powerful, so...so....out of my reach, so different from Gladiator, that I thought I won't be able to work with you. I won't be able to fit in."

Maxim replied "Never change to 'fit-in'. Just be! This place, the cup, will be changed, if need be, to suit you. That reminds me let us have the coffee before it gets cold. Benito will never forgive me if you don't taste it."

Alaska took the gold rimmed cup from Maxim and took a sip of the coffee.

"It tastes different, different but good. What flavor did Benito add?" Alaska asked with a smile.

"I have no idea, but I will convey your comments to Benito. It will make his day" replied Maxim while passing her the cookies.

Alaska picked one and said "Sorry Maxim for reacting the way I did. I was feeling totally overwhelmed with the richness of this place". She softly added "and I was missing Gladiator."

Maxim looked at her piercingly for a moment and then murmured very softly "You, obviously, prefer Gladiator to Maxim. I will have to remember that."

He continued "Do you know why we make our homes, our work places, our cities beautiful - because beauty can arrest us in our tracks, because it hints at something sacred, because it opens a doorway to our True-self for a moment. For a second we get out of our mundane ordinariness and experience the joy of awe inspiring beauty. Beautiful flowers, a painting, music, nature, art, our cosmos, almost anything beautiful, give you a glimpse of your True-self. Aesthetics helps us to do that. And so, we cultivate beauty, but should you find something distasteful here, we shall change it Princess."

Before Alaska could say anything Maxim continued "Now, the last thing that we need to clear away, is money. Do you know Princess, humanity cannot wrap its mind around the fact that there is no lack in the universe, no lack of money, no lack of wealth, health, joy, fun and the greatest of all, it abounds with unconditional love! The limitless energy, in the quantum field of all possibilities, awaits your orders. You choose and it delivers. Humans miss the point that they are conduits for this creative energy to flow through into the 3D world. It flows just as water flows through the tap when you open the faucet of your kitchen sink. When you close the faucet, no water comes, but it does not mean that there is lack of water. Water is not flowing through the tap simply because you have either closed the faucet or forgotten to open it!" Maxim stopped for a moment and offered another cookie to Alaska before continuing.

He said "So, only thing you need to do is open the faucet and let the water flow in your kitchen sink. Princess, I opened the faucet and let wealth flow in my life, to show the world how easily wealth can be manifested! I could never understand why humanity lived in such lack consciousness when they had the power to create anything they could ever think of. So, to follow my vision, I created De Winter Enterprises and money flowed in for the fulfillment of my vision. This particular faucet will be closed the day I sense wealth is no longer required here.

Alaska was listening to him with such rapt attention that she had forgotten to eat the cookie in her hand. Maxim smiled and gently reminded her to eat it if she did not want to disappoint Dorothy, and continued "Princess, you already know money is energy. It has no existence, as such, of its own. If I did not desire it for my vision, it won't be there!"

Alaska, without saying a word, just nodded her head.

Maxim smiled and said "Soon we will visit other offices of De Winter Enterprises and if you do not like them, we will get them changed." Before Alaska could say a word, Maxim added with a quizzing expression in his Indigo eyes "You know, the ones with opulence bordering to vulgarity."

"Hey, I did not say this place was vulgar! Actually I have never seen such a beautiful and stylish office in my life! It is fit for a king!" said Alaska.

"Ah, so it is fit for a king but not for poor Maxim." Said Maxim with a grin, to which Alaska retorted "Poor Maxim indeed! You are fishing for a compliment, aren't you?"

Maxim asked innocently "I am? Such as ….?"

"Such as, everything becomes insignificant in your presence, and you know it!" replied Alaska.

Maxim laughed and said "Princess, if you do not start running now, we will be late for the seminar at the school. You have exactly 5 minutes to wash your hands and be in the car."

CHAPTER 3

Maxim, with Alaska, was on way to Miller High school for the seminar. He was driving the indigo Lamborghini. He looked at Alaska and laughed when he saw her appreciatively touching the dash board of the car.

He said "Hey Princess, you look exactly like a little girl with her new doll!"

Alaska replied "It is a beautiful car. The seats are so soft and comfortable. I like the heavenly smell and the soft music that you always play here, and I love the beautiful Indigo color of the car, the exact color of your eyes!"

Maxim asked "Is that a compliment to me?"

"To you? Well, yes, for owning such a car, and no, the praise was for the car!" replied Alaska with a mischievous smile.

Maxim laughed and said "Alright, I get it."

After a short silence he said "Princess, today at the seminar, I want you to mix with the students and sit with them as audience. Feel and sense their reaction to my presentation. Are they getting it or is it going over their heads. Do they find it boring or are they getting curious about spiritual science. How many present resonate with this and how many are impatiently waiting for the seminar to be over. This is the first thing you will do today. The second, you will give me your feed-back of my presentation. How could I have improved it? What were the short-comings? Where should I have explained in more detail? Any advice to make the presentation more effective would be welcome Princess."

"What? I comment on your presentation? Your presentations are always perfect!" Replied Alaska surprised.

"You want to work with me and help me spread the spiritual knowledge far and wide, don't you? Be critical, not judgmental. It will help me improve and at the same time it will teach you what to say and what not to say when you are yourself presenting a seminar." said Maxim.

There was silence in the car. When Alaska did not say anything Maxim continued "You are going to attend six of my seminars this year. This is the first one. For the remaining five, I will choose seminars at different places with different audiences for you. For the next four, you will sit with the audience and I will present, and for the last one, you will present and I will sit with the audience."

"What? No!" Exclaimed Alaska shocked.

"Yes, Princess, you will! Take this one wish of mine as my command to you. Do it, I know you can. You are not aware of your own deep spiritual knowledge but I am."

Alaska tentatively said "I will try if you think I can ".

Maxim snapped "No, you will not TRY. You will do it! You will present the sixth seminar while I sit with the audience and watch."

There was uncomfortable silence in the car.

Maxim said "All right, let us go back to square one and start all over again. Tell me who you are."

Alaska looked at Maxim. His eyes were fixed on the road.

He repeated "Tell me who you are. Tell me, now."

Alaska began "I am…………."

Maxim interrupted and said "No, hold on. Tell me who you are NOT."

Hearing the question Alaska sat up straight as if a bolt of lightning had hit her. She replied "I am not this physical body. I am not my thoughts, not my emotions, and not my beliefs. So, who am I? I am non-physical, multi-dimensional, boundless awareness, made out of and an expression of the Universe, the Creator. I know I have powers beyond the comprehension of my mind and I also know I am the creator of my reality. I can be, do and have anything that I can think of or ever desire."

Alaska paused for a moment and then shyly added "Thank you for reminding me who I am, and your command will not be disobeyed, I assure you Maxim."

Maxim smiled but said nothing as they had reached the Miller High school where he was invited to speak on spirituality. He parked the car and looked at Alaska. With a smile he gently said "I honor you for saying that."

They were received by Mr. Kennedy, the school principal. After the introductions were over, Maxim, as planned, suggested to the principal that Alaska be allowed to sit with the students as part of the audience. The principal was quite surprised at this. John White, one of the school teachers, showed Alaska the way to the auditorium where the seminar was being held.

Alaska quickly walked into the auditorium without noticing the stares she got from the students. She was dismayed to find the hall full. She started looking for a vacant seat when she was pleasantly surprised by offers of a seat from several students sitting there.

Alaska smiled and said "Thank you. You all are very kind and thoughtful." She sat down on a seat nearest to where she was standing. It turned out to be of a boy who immediately introduced himself as Roger. Alaska told him her name. Roger was very curious. He wanted to know from where she had come, because he was sure he had not seen her in the school earlier.

Alaska told him she was at the university. Roger asked her "Have you come to listen to the famous Gladiator? Why are people crazy about him? Is he really that good?"

Alaska carefully answered "Well, we will have to listen to him first before we can decide whether he is good or not."

"That is true", Roger agreed and eagerly asked "Can I discuss it with you after the seminar is over? You see, I really don't understand these things, but everyone says Gladiator's teachings are very powerful. It can change your life! I would love to become a billionaire like him. "

Alaska gently replied "Sorry, that won't be possible. I have to go back immediately after the seminar. Roger, do find a seat, the seminar is going to begin shortly."

Alaska hoped that will keep Roger silent. She sighed and looked around to gauge the atmosphere, the energetic vibration of the hall. She was disconcerted to see many curious eyes fixed on her. She returned their looks with a gentle smile. After that, Alaska looked straight at the stage and silently said "Hey, Gladiator, come on! Your magnetic presence is urgently required here to engage the attention of the kids. Come now!" And he did!

After the usual introduction and welcome speech by the principal, Maxim stood alone on the stage. He slowly looked around, taking in the vibration of each person present in the hall. He was smiling confidently as usual, but his Indigo eyes had a piercing look. Alaska knew he was seeing everyone through and through.

The boy sitting next to Alaska said in awe "Oh my God." A girl from the front row murmured "WOW!" Someone else said "Can he be a spiritual teacher?" Another commented in surprise "He looks anything but spiritual!" Someone said "He looks like a model to me." Someone else said "So, he is the famous Gladiator. With such looks and the money he is supposed to have, he will, of course, be famous."

Alaska smiled. She wanted to tell the audience that it was not Gladiator's physical attributes, his looks or his wealth, that made him so irresistibly attractive. It was his personal high vibration, and his true desire to awaken every human to their own inherent powers, that made him stand out wherever he went. It was impossible to ignore him or forget him.

Alaska felt the students getting restive, and, as if on cue, Maxim began "Hi, my magicians, I trust you have been flicking your magic wands and creating the life of your dreams out of thin air! I can see the big poster over there boldly announcing "You are the ultimate magician", which, I suppose, has become my signature statement. Well, it is true. You are, but you somehow don't believe it, do you?"

Maxim paused, looked around with a gentle smile and then raised his hand and asked "Anybody who believes it is true? Anyone?"

He looked around. He didn't see any hand raised.

Maxim softly said with a smile "No one?"

And then he saw a small, thin hand raised from somewhere in the middle of the hall. Maxim said "Ah, now I see one. My little friend, could you please stand up so that I can appreciate you better? A mike for my friend, please!"

As soon as the mike reached, a thin, short girl, in a pink shirt, got up with her hand still raised.

Maxim asked her "What makes you think that it is true?"

The girl, without any hesitation, replied "Because you always say it! If it was not true, you would not say it again and again. Something tells me, Gladiator, you never lie!"

"Wow!" Maxim said with a laugh "What a compliment! I will cherish it my friend." He looked around and was surprised to see all hands raised in the auditorium. He smiled and asked "Now, what does this mean?"

The answer came in unison "We too believe it because you believe it Gladiator!"

Maxim looked at his audience with unwavering piercing look in his Indigo eyes and said "I appreciate your courage to speak the truth. So, let us begin."

Maxim asked "Do you know why you find it so difficult to believe that you, like a true magician, can create anything out of thin air, simply by consciously desiring to do so? Well, allow me to tell you. It is because you have been told and you have believed it, all your life, that you do not have the power to do so. That is the crux of the matter. Have you never wondered why you presume that you do not have the power to create the things that you desire? If it is only a belief that you inherited from your family, or from the collective consciousness of the world, what makes you think it is the truth? A belief is only an opinion, not necessarily a truth."

Maxim paused and looked at his young audience. Alaska knew he cared for them and he wanted to ensure they understood basic spiritual law so that they could create a life of their choice.

He began "So, my magicians, for you to be able to believe that you indeed have mind-boggling powers, first, you need to know who you are, who or what you truly are!"

After a short pause, Maxim smiled and continued "yes, I can hear you, my friends, but you have got it wrong. You are not your body, not your name, not your grades, not your thoughts, not your emotions, no nothing! You have a smart phone, but you are not your smart phone, are you? In the same way, you have a body but you are not your body. You, that is, your True-self, inhabit your beautiful body to experience this 3 D physical world through the five senses you have for the purpose. Your body is an electro-magnetic, bio-chemical marvel- appreciate it, love it, take care of it, but it is not you.

So, we are left with the question- what are you? Well, you are non-physical (I prefer to call it beyond physical) boundless awareness or consciousness. You, that is, your True-self, is beyond the limitation of time and space. You are multi-dimensional being. You switch from one dimension to other quite easily and quite often, by changing your vibrational frequency. You are not separate from the Creator. Believe me, you are a perfect expression of our Creator! Actually, I would say you are gods because you have all the potential to experience god-hood just by raising your vibration to align with the energy, that pervades the whole universe and that showers love on one and all equally, without expecting anything in return."

Maxim stopped. There was silence in the hall. Alaska knew that was the effect of Maxim. He captured everyone's imagination and attention, may be, because he always meant what he said. He was genuine through and through.

Maxim resumed "So, now you know, theoretically, what you truly are and thus, how powerful you are. I suggest you write this information on a piece of paper and stick it on your fridge or keep it near your computer or your play-station, or kitchen......etc. where you can see it easily and as often as possible. Slowly this truth will sink in your subconscious. You will start feeling more confident and powerful in unimaginable ways. This change in your belief, of who you are, will change the very chemistry of your physical body. If you wish, you can use the following phrases as affirmations –

I AM the ultimate magician bringing my dreams into existence.

I AM the ultimate creator of my perceived reality.

Maxim stopped again and then said "If you are interested in going deep to learn more and to experience your Self, your True-self that is powerful beyond measure, that you truly are, please contact my website. All information on spirituality and assistance are available there 24/7 for free."

After a short pause he smiled and said "We had started talking about ultimate magicians, didn't we? So, let us find out how you, the magician, can create things you desire out of thin air, so to speak. Shall we?"

There was a chorus of "Yes" from the young audience.

He smiled and continued "I wonder if you have also heard my formula for creating the life of your dreams. Anyway, I will tell you again. It is –

1. Dream.
2. Follow your dream
3. Live the life of your dreams.

Simple, isn't it? So, what do I mean by dream? To dream does not mean you become a couch-potato and keep day-dreaming whole day long munching pop-corns and chips with an inner belief that you can never realize your dreams because you do not have the power to do so. No, that is not what I mean when I ask you to dream.

17

I mean, find out what is it that you would really love to be, to do and to have in your life. What makes you come alive? What are you passionate about? What makes you smile? What thrills you? What can make you jump out of bed early in the morning? I want you to uncover your true desire from deep down your heart and then follow them with unshakable belief that you will achieve it."

Maxim paused for a second and looked at his audience with his usual smile. Then he continued "Not having a dream is not acceptable to me my magicians! Without a dream you become aimless and at best, you will have a mediocre life. Never go through your life like a rudderless ship. You have power beyond measure. Use it to live a life of meaning, of joyful adventure and love."

Maxim paused and looked around till he saw Alaska. He waved and smiled at her. Everyone turned to look at her. She wondered why he did that. Now the students will ask her endless questions about Gladiator.

Maxim resumed "So, the first step is, to ascertain your true desire/dream that makes you come alive. The second step is to follow it. So, how do you follow it? You follow it by feeling happy right now, as if you already have achieved your dream, and never ever, even for a second, doubting the outcome! How do you get this confident? Well, you will become this confident once you believe you are a god with unimaginable immense power to create whatever you desire. You may not believe it but the truth is you have created this moment in your life, whether you like it or dislike it. The process of manifesting your dream is so simple that people find it impossible to believe it, and, because they cannot bring themselves to believe it, they cannot manifest their desire!"

Maxim smiled and asked "Had enough for the day?"

"No" was the answer from the over enthusiastic audience.

Maxim said "Another belief that stops you from manifesting your dream is 'lack'. Trust me, there is nothing like lack in our universe. Let go of this belief if you have been carrying it since your infancy without being aware of it. Believe me, our universe is abundant. There is no lack of money, no lack of joy, no lack of fun, no lack of love, no lack of anything. Then why do some people have lack in their life? Well, because they do not use their imagination to create the abundant life they crave!"

Maxim paused for few seconds and then added "Next thing I want to banish from your psyche is 'fear.' Fear is a kind of matrix that has trapped humanity for centuries. Whenever you feel fear, for whatever reason, ask yourself 'who am I?' Keep asking yourself till you feel energy coursing through your body. You may feel warmth or tingling sensation in your body. Or you may even hear or see or sense your True-self laughing and asking you 'Fear? Fear what? Creator did not create anything more powerful than you. Nothing can harm you, until and unless, you give them the power to do so by believing that they can harm you."

Maxim paused and looked at the eager faces of his young audience and asked "Any questions?"

He waited for a few seconds and then said "No question means everything is clear."

A girl from the second row got up waving her hands. "No, wait. Please wait."

Maxim laughed. A mike was sent to her. She asked "How can I feel I have got something before I have it?"

"Because you are human! As a human you are blessed with the power to imagine a thing which is not in your, so called, reality as yet. If I ask you to imagine a lemon, you can easily do it. You can even experience its lemony taste without having a slice of lemon in your mouth! So, first think about the thing you desire, then imagine it in detail, then visualize it and the last and the most important, feel it in your body! Feel the joy of having it, before it actually is, in 3D reality. It is easy to do and as a matter of fact, you do it quite often without being aware." replied Maxim.

He paused for a little while, giving the audience time to question him. When there was no question he continued "I am quite sure, some of you, if not all, must be enjoying games using computer augmented reality and/or virtual reality and getting totally immersed in the experience. Haven't you? It would be quite interesting if you would create computer programs that could give you the feeling and/or experience of the thing you want to manifest in your life. It would be a fun way to experience your dream before it has manifested in your physical reality. Of course, it is not necessary to use these AR or VR programs to experience your dream before it manifests. Your powerful imagination can do it for you."

After a short pause Maxim continued "All this talk about imagination reminds me of our universe. I trust you know everything is energy, energy vibrating at its own particular frequency, and what you see with your eyes, is the interpretation of your mind of the actual energy waves vibrating there. In old wisdom traditions it was said that our universe was a 'Maya', an illusion, a kind of virtual reality simulation, a 'Leela', a game being played by God. So, my magicians, what do you say – are you ready to continue playing the game by manifesting your dreams?"

The response from the excited audience was a roar of 'Yes'.

Alaska smiled hearing the enthusiastic reply.

"So, what is stopping you? Believe me, you are the master creator of all you perceive" asked Maxim.

A boy stood up with his hands waving to draw Maxim's attention. When he got the mike he said "But it does not work for me! I know what I want but I cannot manifest it."

Maxim laughed and said "You are the sovereign. Believe it! When you place an order with the universe for your 'dream', it will be delivered in its perfect time. It never gets lost in the mail my friend. Either you have placed an order for a wrong thing, a thing that you actually don't want, or you have given a wrong address for the thing to be delivered at. Release all ideas that the divine force of creation, the un-seen world of quantum field where anything is possible, does not work for you. Just as the force of gravity is always working, whether you believe it or not, so is the force of creation always creating and creating the precise thing you ordered, whether you believe it or not! Banish the thought that you need to be someone special or you need to do something special before your 'dream' manifests. Let go of all disempowering limiting beliefs right now! Feel excited and thrilled that your 'dream' has already manifested in your reality. Shout yoo-hoo, run, jump and dance with the joy of your 'dream' coming true!"

After a short pause Maxim asked "Could you again stand up my friend so that I can read you better, or still better, could you come over here?"

The boy stood up but didn't move. He looked nervous. After nearly a minute, he surprised everyone by walking up to the stage and standing right in front of Maxim. Maxim smiled and said "Look up my friend! Now!"

There was silence in the hall.

After looking piercingly at the boy, Maxim said "Your life has changed in the un-seen quantum field where anything is possible, where all your desires are waiting for your command to manifest, even instantaneously, if you can change your belief in an instant!"

Maxim paused, looking at the boy with a quizzical expression in his Indigo eyes.

Suddenly the boy said "I can make it happen. I feel my 'dream' has come true! Gladiator, has it? I am excited. I am so happy you came to our school! Thank you, thank you, thank you! Are you really a magician Gladiator?"

Maxim gently said in a voice that touched everyone "Yes, I am and so are you! Believe me, you are an ultimate magician. You too play with cosmic forces to create a world of your dreams as I do."

There was pin-drop silence as if the audience was waiting for Gladiator to say something more. When Maxim waved to the audience before leaving the stage, the audience came to life with a thunderous applause. Maxim kept waving to the kids for some time and then as he moved towards the exit, someone shouted "Don't go! We want Gladiator!" And then hundreds of students joined in shouting "We want Gladiator! We want Gladiator!" And then, above the din someone shouted "We love Gladiator". And of course then everyone picked that up and shouted "We love Gladiator! We love Gladiator!"

Alaska realized she was laughing and shouting with everyone else "We love Gladiator!" There was something in Maxim that touched the core of one's being. It awakened one to break free from artificial inhibitions and feel totally free to express oneself. Alaska knew it was so because Maxim himself was like that-totally authentic, in total integrity and radiating the divine love for the whole creation.

Alaska saw someone hand over a mike to Maxim. Maxim shouted "And Gladiator loves you my ultimate magicians!"

There was an appreciative roar from the audience but the chant went on "We love Gladiator!"

The school principal with some teachers came on the stage and escorted Gladiator out of the auditorium through a side door.

CHAPTER 4

As soon as Maxim left the stage Alaska quickly moved towards the nearest exit, but, obviously she was not quick enough. The passage was already packed with students, trying to exit the hall. Alaska had no option but to walk slowly with the crowd when Roger caught up with her.

He said "Hi Alaska! Did you like the seminar?"

Alaska asked "What about you? Did you like it?"

Roger murmured "Let me come in front. I will have you out of the auditorium in five minutes."

And he kept his word. He kept pulling and pushing people clearing a path from Alaska and in a few minutes they were outside the hall.

Alaska thanked Roger and quickly moved towards the car park where Maxim had left the Lamborghini, hoping Roger would take the hint and not follow her, but, alas, it was not to be! When she looked back over her shoulder, Alaska was dismayed to see, not only Roger, but a crowd of students following her. She kept walking as quickly as she could till she saw the Lamborghini. Questions were pouring. Before she could answer one, there were five more. "Did you like the seminar?" "Do you believe Gladiator?" "Is it true anything is possible if we believe it?" "How do you dream?" "Why does Gladiator say we are magicians?" "How can you follow your dream?" "How do you know Gladiator?" "Where did you meet him?" "Can you introduce me to him?" "Does he have coaching classes?" Questions went on pouring. Alaska thought of Maxim for a second. What would he have done? She stopped walking and turned towards the crowd that had been following her. She took a slow breath, relaxed and asked the students with a gentle smile "If you expect an answer, you have to wait for it. Hmm..?" Alaska was not aware of her magnetic presence that made the students follow her.

By this time, Maxim had reached his car with the school principal and a few others. He took in the scene around Alaska. He thanked the principal and said "My friend needs rescuing. Excuse me." Saying this he walked towards Alaska. When he reached her, he gently put his arm around her shoulder and slightly pulled her towards himself. Alaska was surprised but before she could say a word Maxim said with his usual smile "All answers that you seek are at the website. Open it, have fun with it and create the life of your dreams. Believe me, each one of you is an ultimate magician!" Saying this Maxim guided Alaska to the car, opened the door for her and then went round the front of the car and got in behind the wheel. As he shut the door, Alaska asked "Why did you put your arm around my shoulder in that.......familiar way, in front of the kids? Were you trying to give them hints to keep their distance from me?"

Hearing this, Maxim, who had switched on the car, switched it off and turned towards Alaska. He looked at her with an unfathomable expression, without his usual smile. He kept looking at her as if he was searching for an answer in her face.

After a few seconds of silence, Maxim said "No! That is not true Princess. OK, time to go" and switched on the car. With amusement in his voice he added "Time to give your dazzling smile to your ardent fans Princess."

Alaska looked out and gasped. It seemed the whole school was there to see them off. Maxim smiled, rolled down the windows and waved to the waiting crowd. Alaska smiled and waved at them as Maxim drove out of the school parking lot.

There was silence except for the soft music playing in the car.

After a minute or so Maxim asked "Could you direct me to a restaurant in or around your university campus where we can have dinner in peace?"

Alaska looked at him and said "In peace, in the campus? Are you kidding? Everyone knows you. You will end up conducting a seminar and treating a dozen or so to burgers as well!"

Maxim softly said "That won't do. You have yet to give your report, the feed-back about today's seminar. Let me think where I can take you, where we can eat and talk undisturbed."

After a moment he said "It is a bit far from your dorm but we can eat and talk there."

Alaska asked "Where are we going?"

"To my hotel" replied Maxim "Their coffee shop is quite spacious and I believe they serve good burgers, if that is what you would like to eat. You better keep your fingers crossed lest we meet someone who believes I know him and start a conversation with the state of the weather in Honolulu!"

Alaska couldn't stop laughing. She asked "What? Is that what people do as an excuse to talk with you?

"Not all and not always, but quite often." replied Maxim with a smile.

Soon they reached the hotel. Maxim gave the key to the valet to park his car. They went in and Maxim quickly guided Alaska to the coffee shop. When they entered, the coffee shop appeared to be completely full. Just then, a waiter rushed over to them and said "Good evening Mr. De Winter. A table for two? Far from the madding crowd? Sir?"

Maxim smiled and said "Yes Ronny, you have got it right."

The waiter led them to a table near a small fountain in the middle of the coffee shop. He gave them the wine list and asked "What would you like this evening Sir, madam?"

Maxim looked at Alaska for a moment and said "I don't need any artificial stimulation this evening Ronny. Water will suffice."

"Madam?" the waiter prompted Alaska.

"Could I have iced lemon tea, please?" Alaska asked.

"Sure madam" the waiter said. Before he could leave, Maxim said "and something to eat for my friend here, Ronny."

"Sure sir, I will get the menu" replied the waiter, to which Maxim said "No need to bring the menu. The other day you were talking about a very special burger created by your chef. Let us try that today."

"Yes sir. It really is good. You will like it." He looked at Alaska. Alaska said she would also have the same. The waiter looked a little doubtful and said "I hope you like fruits and vegetables. It is a meatless burger, Madam."

"Is it? I will try it, all the same." replied Alaska with her beautiful smile. Ronny stopped for a second and looked at her. After a moment he said "Very well, madam, you will not regret it." Saying this, as he turned to go, Maxim added "and don't forget to get a basket of French fries Ronny" to which Alaska added with a big smile "Could it be possible to have potato wedges instead of fries, Ronny?"

Ronny stopped in his tracks to stare at Alaska. He quickly recovered and softly said "Yes, madam, of course." and went away.

Alaska suddenly realized that Maxim was laughing his head off.

Alaska asked "Why are you laughing?"

When Maxim could stop laughing, he said "Poor Ronny. You gave him the shock of his life with your dazzling smile. Anyway, be prepared to eat at least two baskets of potato wedges. If Ronny could, he would have half the potatoes of the town made into wedges for you."

"Maxim, you are deliberately making fun of me, aren't you? And yes, that reminds me, why you always say 'get the cookies or get the burger for my friend', as if I am a little girl, always hungry." complained Alaska.

"Aren't you?" softly asked Maxim.

"What?" asked Alaska.

"Hungry". Replied Maxim with a little smile.

"No, I am not!" replied Alaska with a frown.

Maxim murmured gently "No?"

"Well, yes, I am hungry. I have had nothing to eat after the cookies that Dorothy brought at your office." Alaska grudgingly accepted.

Maxim kept looking at Alaska with a gentle smile and then murmured "your spontaneous reactions are enchanting to watch Princess. I wonder if you know how enchanting it is!"

Alaska asked "What? What did you say? I can hardly hear you Maxim."

Maxim got up and pulled his chair to the side of the table near Alaska's chair saying "Yes, the table is too wide to talk across it. Now we can hear each other. Alright, now, tell me your views about the seminar or rather your views about my presentation, to be more precise."

Before Alaska could start their food arrived and Ronny did bring two baskets, one full of French fries and the other full of potato wedges along with their burgers and iced tea for her.

Maxim murmured "As expected!"

Before Ronny could launch into an explanation about the two baskets, Maxim quickly said "Thank you Ronny" and started eating.

Alaska appreciated her huge plate of burger decorated colorfully with fruits and vegetables. She started eating without any further talk.

After a few minutes Maxim asked "Like it Princess?"

Alaska nodded her head and said "It is good. What about you? Did you like it?"

"Yes. I did. I think both of us were hungry, after all." replied Maxim with a smile.

When they had finished eating and Alaska was sipping her remaining iced-tea, Maxim said "We got side-tracked by the burgers Princess. Do you think you can now give me your feed- back on my presentation?"

Alaska thought for a moment and then said "Maxim, you didn't tell the students why they should ask 'who am I?' You could have explained that by repeatedly asking this they will become aware of and gradually connect with their True-self, the inner magician where the power is to create miracles. I think they would have enjoyed it."

After a short pause Alaska continued "And Maxim, why don't you tell them up-front that they need to know their own power, both theoretically and experientially. They must own the power and acknowledge it before they can use it. Isn't that true Maxim? And if they don't accept their own tremendous power, how will they push through the inertia of their comfort zone that keeps them stagnating in an unhappy life day-in and day-out?"

Maxim reached out his hand to tuck a strand of hair behind Alaska's ear. He kept running his fingers gently through her hair.

Alaska said "Hey Maxim! You are not listening!" She realized Maxim's Indigo eyes were on her face, but there was a far- away look in them. She gently removed his hands from her hair and asked "Where are you? What are you doing?"

Slowly Maxim replied "I am listening to you. I can repeat word-by-word of what you just said. And, where am I? Well, I am with the most beautiful woman, with the most beautiful silky hair, and I am messing it up with my chubby hands and she is looking at me with brilliant Indigo eyes full of love and oh, so indulgent and ...." Maxim suddenly stopped.

Alaska felt a twinge of pain in her heart. Softly she asked "Your mother, Maxim?"

Maxim nodded and murmured "I wonder what it is. May be it is your silky hair or is it the gentle expression in your eyes or could it be your beautiful smile that reminds me of Angelina, my mother."

After a short pause he continued "I have never felt a desire to physically touch anything or anybody. Actually, I have been quite happy and satisfied acting from and remaining focused in the non-physical realm until now. I am really surprised at this urge to physically touch."

When he kept quiet Alaska prompted "touch what?"

Maxim smiled and said "You!"

Alaska felt herself turning pink.

Maxim laughed and said "Time to take you back to your campus, little one!"

CHAPTER 5

Alaska was walking back from the library when her phone rang. She saw it was from Maxim. She said "Hi Maxim! When are you coming to Boston?"

Maxim replied "Soon. Where are you Princess?"

"In the campus" replied Alaska.

"Precisely where in the campus?" asked Maxim.

Alaska asked "Why? Are you here Maxim?"

"Very near you. If you give me your exact location, I will treat you tonight to a Chinese dinner. How does that sound?" said Maxim.

Alaska asked "What? Are you kidding Maxim?"

"Hold on." replied Maxim.

Alaska looked around. She was thrilled to see Maxim's Indigo Lamborghini slowing to a halt across the road. She sprinted across the road and hurled herself onto Maxim who had just got out of the car. Maxim caught her in a bear hug. Alaska asked him "Why didn't you tell me you were coming here today?"

Maxim, without saying a word, kept holding her in his arms. Alaska didn't know for how long they stood like that on the sidewalk. When Maxim loosened his arms, Alaska looked up and gently asked "Maxim, what is wrong?"

Maxim looked at her for a few seconds. "Nothing is wrong. I didn't inform you because I was not sure if I will be able to catch this flight and be here to take you for dinner tonight." Maxim replied with a smile.

Alaska asked when they got in the car "Where are you coming from Maxim and where are you going after the dinner?"

Maxim laughed and said, while navigating the car though the traffic "First you tell me how your work is coming along? And the meditation, and the spiritual practices. How easily and for how long can you hold super consciousness? And I hope you will complete your Masters as soon as possible, won't you Princess?"

Alaska said "No, first you answer me. I feel uncomfortable, when I am half through the dinner you get a reminder call informing you that your flight is now boarding."

"No, it won't happen because I am not leaving tonight." gently replied Maxim.

"You are not? Good. I can relax." After a moment she added "Not tonight, that means you are leaving tomorrow? Tomorrow morning?"

Maxim nodded and asked her "So, what would you prefer-Chinese or something else?"

Alaska replied "Anything will do." She shyly added "I can hardly believe you are here. I am so happy Maxim!"

"So am I Princess! Your exuberance has an energy field that spans my whole world!" softly replied Maxim.

It took them nearly 15 minutes to reach the restaurant. It looked nice with Chinese paintings and gold and pink lanterns hanging over the tables. They were seated at a table near the window. Whenever Alaska went anywhere with Maxim, people stopped to look at them and this evening was no exception. Everyone paused for a second and looked at them. Alaska tried to remain oblivious as Maxim always was.

Maxim asked Alaska to check the menu and order, but Alaska said "You choose."

Maxim looked in her eyes for a few seconds and then quickly ordered, from the starter to the dessert, in one go and dismissed the petite girl taking the order by saying "That will be all. Thank you."

When the girl left, Alaska laughed out loud.

Maxim looked at her and asked with a smile "What is so funny? Did you want to order something else?"

Alaska replied "No, I didn't want to order. What I find funny is the way you ordered the whole dinner in less than a minute and then quickly, without any further ado, dismissed her by saying 'that will be all. Thank you.' You didn't give her a chance to suggest or discuss their "specialties"! I think they and the diners enjoy doing that."

Maxim replied "I don't want to waste my time talking with her. I am clear on that." After a moment he asked "Tell me are you enjoying doing Masters in astrophysics? What are the new scientific discoveries that excite you?"

Alaska thought for a moment and then launched into her favorite subject, her eyes shining with enthusiasm. She kept talking, interspersed by questions from Maxim, till their food was served.

After some time Maxim asked "How are your friends who wanted to meet me but always missed me?"

Alaska laughed and said "All of them have moved away. I miss them. We keep in touch mostly through phone, and they still want to meet you."

Maxim thoughtfully replied "I cannot meet them in these short visits, but I will make a longer stopover, one of these days and treat them to lunch or dinner."

"Oh, that would be great! Maxim, do you remember James? You repaid half of his students' loan. He really wants to meet you and thank you. No, not for repaying his loan, but for doing something that totally changed him and his life."

Maxim asked "Would you like me to repay his complete loan?"

Alaska replied with a smile "James won't let you do that now. He is a changed person. He is confident and happy with goals, visions and mission Maxim!"

Alaska continued "Most of my present class mates seem to be quite serious about their studies and focused on their future careers. Maxim, there is a boy in my class, a French boy, who is always staring at me. There is something about him that seems familiar, that reminds me of someone. His name is Jacque."

Maxim stopped eating and asked "What?"

Alaska repeated "Jacque." She was quite surprised at Maxim's reaction to the name. She asked "Do you know him?"

"No, I don't think so. Does the name, Jacque, reminds you or is it his face that reminds you of someone?" asked Maxim looking closely at Alaska.

Alaska thought for a moment and replied "I.....I don't know. He makes me feel sad a kind of forgotten ache comes up in my heart Maxim."

Maxim reached out and held her hands and said "Let us forget him and enjoy our food Princess."

Alaska looked at him and asked "Could you see something?"

Maxim nodded but didn't say anything. He asked her to taste the dessert. Obviously he was trying to change the subject. Alaska knew he will tell her when the time was right. Oh, well, why am I thinking of Jacque when Maxim was here with her.

With a bright smile Alaska asked "Maxim, why do you use the name 'Gladiator' for your spiritual work?"

Maxim smiled and asked "Do you really want to know?"

Alaska replied "Well, yes. Is it a secret?"

Maxim ruefully said "No, it is not a secret but not complimentary to me. It originated in the ego of a little boy."

He paused for a moment and then began "OK, here is the story. When as a little boy I came to live with Martin, my father's elder brother, my mind was full of magic, angels, sword fighters, Samurai...etc. It could be, quite possibly, hints from my True-self to my conscious mind that I was different in many ways, that I had powers that others may think magical. Anyway, to cut the long story short, Martin started calling me 'Merlin, the magician'. When I asked him why he called me Merlin, he explained that Merlin was the greatest magician of all times on Earth. Well, I was satisfied with that explanation till the day I saw a picture of Merlin in a new book. He was depicted as a stooping old man with long grey beard touching the very ground he was standing on!"

Maxim laughed and then continued "I was furious. I marched to Martin's study and threw the book at his head. Thank God, he ducked and was not hurt. I showed him the picture of Merlin in the book and shouted 'do I look like that?' Poor Martin, he gently said 'No, but Merlin was the greatest magician ever'. That didn't help much. It couldn't calm the hurt ego of young Maxim. So, Martin, after some thought selected a book on Roman Empire from his library and showed him a picture of a Gladiator with a sword in his hand and with muscular arms and legs. A very impressive figure indeed! After showing the picture of the handsome gladiator, Martin told the young boy that starting now, he will call him Gladiator because that is how he will look when he grows up, and the little boy grudgingly accepted."

Alaska couldn't stop laughing. She said "Maxim, did you know I did not want to come to your seminar, the first time you had come to our university? I was skeptical of a person who called himself 'Gladiator'. I had sarcastically asked Mark, who was trying to persuade me to attend the seminar, if you looked like a Roman Gladiator! And I didn't go with them to the auditorium, but curiosity got the better of me, and I finally checked your website and was startled to see a pair of Indigo eyes staring at me from a photo at the bottom of the page. Something snapped inside me. I thought you smiled at me, and I started running to the auditorium hoping to catch the closing of the seminar, but of course, instead, I literally crashed into you."

Maxim laughed and said "Yes, you did! Olympic race was on!"

Alaska smiled and asked "So, it was Martin who called you Gladiator. But why do you still use the name for all your spiritual work?"

Maxim remained silent for some time lost in old memories. Then he began "Martin passed away when I had just joined college. A week before his death he called me and said that he had left an envelope with our attorney with the instruction that it be handed over to me on my 27th birthday. He had requested me to follow the instruction that he had given for me in the letter. He had added 'I know you can do it my Gladiator'. Of course I had asked him 'Why don't you give the instructions now?'

He had replied with hint of a smile 'Because I want to give some more time to your conscious mind, to grasp the enormity of having your immense knowledge and spiritual powers my son, even though you are not aware of it, at the moment, I know your un-told powers. I know you can easily do what I want you to do, Gladiator, my son!'

After a short pause he continued "On the morning of my 27th birthday I got a call from my attorney that he would be coming to personally deliver a letter to me. He came and handed over Martin's letter to me, and that was the beginning of my seminars, presentations, spiritual school, and the website with all possible information on spirituality. Martin had asked me to do it because he thought now was the perfect time for a spiritual renaissance. It was time for people to re-discover spirituality in the correct form. He thought this knowledge should be used by everyone to live happier lives. And yes, it was Martin's expressed desire that I do this work under the banner of, or name of, Gladiator."

Maxim stopped for a moment and then said with a smile "The end! End of the story."

Alaska, who had been listening with rapt attention, exclaimed "Oh, wow, what a story!" She hesitated for a second, then asked "Maxim, you cared for Martin, didn't you?"

Maxim nodded without saying a word.

"Oh, Maxim, can I ask you one more question?" asked Alaska.

"Sure. Some coffee?" asked Maxim.

Alaska nodded her head and shyly asked "Why do you always call me Princess?"

"You don't like it?" asked Maxim. His brilliant Indigo eyes were fixed on her.

Alaska replied "Of course I like it!" She softly added "I love it when you say 'your wish is my command Princess'."

Maxim smiled and kept looking at her with an intense expression in his beautiful eyes. He didn't say a word. Just then their coffee arrived and Alaska felt relieved when Maxim shifted his gaze from her face to the coffee. After the waiter had left, Maxim replied "Not now Princess. It is not the right time. I will tell you later."

Alaska looked disappointed. Maxim smiled and said "Now, you tell me something. Is there any special reason, for your name 'Alaska'?"

Alaska replied "Well, yes. My parents wanted to have a child but they couldn't. For years they tried. Then one day my Mom said 'this is enough, no more trying.' Saying this she went out and looked at the star studded night sky and said aloud 'Let thy will be done!' Next day they left for Alaska for their annual vacation and ...."

"........and you came along! What a perfect time you chose Princess to descend from your heavenly abode to Earth."

Alaska smiled and nodded her head.

Suddenly Maxim asked her "Would you like to go to Alaska for a seminar?"

"What? Alaska? Oh, I will love it. Are you going there?" asked Alaska.

Maxim replied "Actually I was not planning to go there, but why not? More work for Brian, Brent and Dorothy. They will juggle with my schedule and somehow include a weekend in Alaska, a weekend so that you don't miss your classes."

"Oh, Maxim, when are you going there? Can I really come along?" Alaska asked all excited about the proposed trip.

"Sure! When? – I am not sure. Tomorrow I will ask Brian and others to reschedule my meetings to include a trip to Alaska. I will let you know the date as soon as possible." Maxim replied.

"Do let me know soon so that I can make my flight and hotel reservation." Alaska said with a big smile.

"You need not worry about flight and hotel reservations. Dorothy will do it. I think, most probably you will be traveling on a Friday night to Anchorage and back some time on Sunday."

"Is the seminar in Anchorage or somewhere else? Do you know the people who have invited you?" asked Alaska.

"Well, it is somewhere near Denali National Park. We will drive to the Resort, and the hosts are a group of people who call themselves 'Senior citizens'. They have been asking for the seminar for more than a year. They have threatened that if, I cannot come for this seminar, they will march to Gladiator's school and sit there till I personally answer all their queries. My videos and Holographic presentations have been sent to them but they are not satisfied. They want my physical presence." Maxim replied.

"I don't blame them. Your physical presence is something extraordinary. I wonder if you know the kind of energy you radiate. You simply blast your audience with your own raw power Maxim!"

Maxim looked at Alaska with a gentle smile and said "Don't get too attached to this physical form Princess. What you see, is the interpretation of your mind of my vibration, not the reality. Attachment to any physical form gives rise to fear, fear of losing it. Tell me Princess, today when I came to your campus to pick you up, did you see a car coming from behind you when you ran across the road?"

"Was there a car coming? No, I didn't see it. I was thrilled to see you!" said Alaska.

Maxim spoke very slowly "Today, for the first time in my life I experienced fear. It took me quite a while to get back my balance and to remember that we are only playing a game, creating a story, a cinema, in our limitless awareness and, that I cannot lose you, that I will never lose the True-you, Princess!"

When Maxim stopped, Alaska said "Sorry. Sorry Maxim, I really didn't see the car. Er... is that why you held me for so long and almost crushed me?" she added with a twinkle in her eyes.

Maxim laughed and said "Did I? Forgive me, but I need to speak with your mother and ask her to teach you again what to do before running across a road- look to the right, then look to the left and then again look to the right, or is it the other way round?"

Alaska laughed and said "Of course I know the rules!"

Maxim looked at his watch, asked for the bill and said "Time for the little-one to be in bed Let us go."

CHAPTER 6

Alaska had just finished her lunch when she got a call from her mother. She said "Hi Mom! I was just going to call you. How is everything there?"

Her mother replied "Black Rose is not keeping well. The vet has seen her. He said she should be ok soon. This time when you come home you must see her. She misses you, as I do."

"Oh, Mom I miss you too!" Alaska replied.

Her mother said "I had called to inform you that next Saturday we are getting Gladiator's next Holographic presentation at the club. Do come over. His presentations are always interesting, if nothing else. Of course I find them enlightening."

Alaska said "Oh, Mom, I may not be able to come because I may be going to Alaska on Friday returning on Sunday. I did not tell you because it is not confirmed as yet."

Her mother asked "Alaska? That should be fun. Who are you going with? Have you enough funds to cover the cost of your ticket, hotel and other expenses? Don't forget to take your woolen jacket. It gets quite cold there."

"Mom, Maxim is going there for a seminar. He has asked me to attend it as part of my training. He will receive me at Anchorage airport, and then we drive to the venue of the seminar near Denali. He presents in the evening of Saturday. I am supposed to sit with the audience and listen and learn. We stay the night at the resort and depart on Sunday morning for Anchorage so that I am back in Boston in time for my Monday classes."

There was silence on the line. Then her mother asked "Didn't you attend Gladiator's seminar last month?"

Alaska replied "Yes. I did. That was the first of a total of six seminars I am supposed to attend this year Mom."

"What do you mean Aly?" Her mother asked sounding a bit worried.

Alaska explained "You see Mom, Maxim asked me to attend six of his seminars this year. For the first five, he will present and I will listen sitting with the audience. The last one, the sixth seminar, I am supposed to present while Maxim will sit with the audience and listen. He is sure I can do it. Of course he makes me practice and work for it. In Alaska he is presenting to a group called 'senior citizen'. Maxim has asked me to prepare for this seminar as if I was going to present it. The last seminar I attended, among other things, Maxim made me tell him how he could have improved his presentation. Every time I meet him Mom I learn something new. He is amazing!"

"Oh, Aly, my little girl, I am proud of you. You have always been brilliant but presenting a seminar on spirituality like Gladiator is difficult to envision, but, if Gladiator says you can, then you can. Let me give the news to Joe. Call me when everything is finalized."

****

Alaska was thrilled at the prospect of going to Denali for the seminar with Maxim. An hour ago, she had got a call from Dorothy asking her to be prepared to leave for Anchorage coming Friday night. She will be sending all details in an email to her. And now she was excitedly awaiting the email from Dorothy.

Just then her father called. Alaska said "Hi Dad, how are you?"

Her father said "Little one, I am excited. Mom gave me the news. When will you be presenting your first seminar? Let us know as soon as possible so that we can be there and sit with Gladiator and the audience."

"Oh, Dad, I don't know. This Alaska one is the second seminar I will be attending."

"Alright. Let me have all the details along with the cost for the flight, hotel etc. Hope you have chosen flights with sufficient time gap between the connecting flights to Anchorage or would you like me to do it for you?"

Alaska replied "Thank you Dad, but I know nothing about the flights as Dorothy has done it and I am awaiting her email with all details."

"Dorothy? Who is she?" Her father asked.

"Dad, she is the lady who makes all reservations for Maxim. She had called me an hour ago and told me that I should be ready to take the flight on Friday night."

"Gladiator has not spoken with you about this trip to Alaska?" Her father asked surprised.

"Not today, Dad. He had asked me some fifteen days ago when he was in Boston last. Right now he is somewhere in Europe." replied Alaska.

There was a short pause and then he said "Well, let me know the details as soon as you receive this email from the lady, and I have a suggestion little one, do not board the flight to Anchorage till Gladiator himself calls you and asks you to come, again."

Alaska quickly said "Dad, don't misunderstand Maxim. He really is very busy, crossing the globe several times a month. Do you know why Dad? He does it so that others can live happier lives! And Dad I should tell you something more right now. I will ask him about the cost of the trip to Alaska because you want me to. Personally, now, money doesn't bother me. Dad, when I first went to the De Winter Enterprises local office here, I was hit hard by the realization that Maxim was not from our world. I had known that he was rich, but not that rich, that powerful! I had seen him as Gladiator, gentle, kind, always smiling but there he appeared overwhelmingly different. This Maxim looked the billionaire that he is who controlled the empire of De Winter Enterprises effortlessly around the world. And Dad, I told him that, that day in his office. And Maxim had asked 'Does it matter? I thought only I mattered to you, not the outer trappings!' Oh dad, to cut the long story short, that day I realized what actually mattered was Maxim, only Maxim, Maxim the man, the spiritual teacher, or in whatever way you perceived him. Nothing else mattered. Money is energy just like everything else. We open the faucet and money flows and it stops when we close the faucet."

After a short silence her father said "Thanks little one. Give me time to digest what you just said. I respect Gladiator, but it is you, only you, that matter to me. Your happiness is of paramount importance to me, little one! Bless you!"

"Oh Dad, I love you!" Alaska said before disconnecting the phone.

****

Alaska was on board the flight to Anchorage. She was so excited she could not close her eyes. Other passengers were already dozing after the dinner. Alaska was feeling relieved after telling Maxim on the phone about her father wanting to know the total cost of the trip to Alaska. Maxim had promised he will speak with her father on their arrival in Denali. Alaska took out her note pad and started writing down things she would say to the 'senior citizen' group, that is, if she had to present the seminar. She was surprised as ideas flowed effortlessly to her mind. But where it was coming from, she wondered. After a couple of hours of noting her ideas, she finally dozed off and slept. She woke up when the breakfast was being served just before landing in Anchorage. She remembered she was going to meet Maxim in an hour or so. He had said his flight lands an hour earlier than hers, so he will be there to receive her at the airport.

Alaska's flight was on time. She eagerly went inside the airport hoping to see Maxim, but couldn't find him. She collected her suitcase. Still, no Maxim. Then she went to check the flight arrivals and saw that Maxim's flight was delayed. It would be landing in five minutes. She knew it will take Maxim at least twenty minutes, if not more, to meet her. She was wondering what to do next when she became aware of a man talking to her "I have been watching you for some time. Are you waiting for someone?"

Alaska said "Yes" and started walking towards the row of shops. The man followed her. He said "I am also waiting for my friends. They should be here soon to pick me up. I am called Allen." Saying this he reached for her hand to shake it.

Alaska looked at him. She saw un-washed face, dirty nails, disreputable clothes that had never been washed, or at least it appeared to be so. She involuntarily turned away from him mumbling 'my friend has come'. Alaska desperately wished for Maxim to come.

She looked around and was over-joyed to see him waving from quite a distance. She ran towards him pulling her suitcase and dodging other passengers. Maxim hugged her and said "Forgive me for not being here to receive you. Let us move to the side."

He guided her to one side and asked "What caused the Olympic race?"

Alaska laughed and said "I was happy to see you."

"So am I Princess. It is as well you don't know how much. But the Olympic race- what were you running away from?" asked Maxim.

Alaska thought for a moment, then, said "I was running away from that guy." She was surprised to see the man still standing there staring at her.

"What happened? Did he misbehave?" asked Maxim looking keenly at her.

Alaska replied "No. That makes me feel worse, makes me feel almost guilty. You see, he introduced himself and reached for my hand to shake it and …..then I saw him! His unwashed face, his dirty clothes, his hands with dirty nails! I just couldn't let him touch me, so I ran, and then I saw you! I know Maxim he is just like you and me, we are all connected, expression of our one creator, but why do they live in this filthy fashion?"

Maxim tucked a strand of hair behind her ear and said "Don't feel guilty at all! He deserved it."

He looked at the man once and said "Come, I will buy you a cappuccino and then look for our car that will take us to the Resort in Denali."

They found their car driver near the airport exit. As they were walking towards the car Maxim said to Alaska "There is your man with dirty nails. Would you like to give him a chance to a cleaner, happier life?"

Alaska saw the man chatting with another man and two girls, all as disreputable as he was.

She asked "What do you mean."

"Princess, people dress and live in this fashion to defy the norms of society. They want to be approved by the world but believe they are not good enough and so, they go to the other extreme daring the society to criticize them. They need to be told who they truly are, how magnificent they are, that they are gods!" replied Maxim.

"What can we do?" asked Alaska.

Maxim took out a few folders and colorful notices for the evening seminar from his briefcase and said "You can give these to the man and ask him and his friends to attend the seminar. May be they will hear something that will change their lives."

Alaska looked at the man and his friends and said "You give it to him."

Maxim laughed and said "I promise I won't let him touch you. Shall we?"

Alaska nodded her head. They walked towards the group. Maxim put his arm around Alaska's shoulder, drawing her closer to him and gave her the pamphlets for the seminar. Alaska was doubtful but cheerfully said "Hi Allen, I am going to attend this seminar. Will you come?"

Allen stopped talking. Four pairs of eyes stared at her. The girl in a long red dress recovered first and asked "What is it?" She took the pamphlets from Alaska.

Maxim smiled and said "It is a seminar that I will be presenting this evening. I will be talking about how to fearlessly create the life of your dreams."

The girl stared at Maxim for a few seconds, then, said "Yes. Yes I would like to come" She asked others "Are you three coming?"

They looked at the pamphlets and said "It is not here. It is in Denali."

Maxim said "Yes. You can drive or take a bus. It takes a few hours to reach Denali. We are going to drive."

"Are you? Hey guys, let us go." The other girl, who had been silently looking at Maxim, said with a smile.

Alaska thought for a moment and said, from the safety of Maxim's arms around her shoulder "Come Allen. It would be fun!"

Allen asked Alaska "Are you going? Will you be there?"

Alaska nodded her head.

"OK, we will come but at least tell me your name. I don't even know your name." said Allen.

Maxim softly said "Alaska."

Allen said "What?"

Maxim smiled and said "You heard it friend. She is called Alaska, difficult to forget."

Allen kept looking at Alaska for some time. Then he said "Alaska. Alaska, I will never forget you."

Alaska and Maxim left them and went to the car. They sipped their coffee which was lukewarm by now, as they drove to Denali.

Maxim asked Alaska "Would you like me to talk with your Dad now? There won't be much free time later."

Alaska exclaimed "Oh, I forgot to telephone Mom. She had asked me to call her as soon as I landed in Anchorage." She was taking out her phone when it started ringing. It was her mother. Alaska said "Hi Mom! I was just going to call you."

Her mother asked "How are you? Has Gladiator arrived?"

Alaska said "Yes, Mom, he is here. Mom is Dad there? Maxim would like to speak with him."

Alaska gave the phone to Maxim saying "He is coming."

After a short silence Maxim said "Good morning Mr. Ashley. Yes, Alaska is fine. We are in the car driving to Denali National Park. Mr. Ashley, Alaska told me you would like to know the cost of her air fare and for her stay at the resort in Denali. Well, as a matter of fact, I don't know the exact amount because all these arrangements are done by my office, but if you really want it, I will check and let you know. Mr. Ashley, I have a request. Could you please grant me the pleasure of treating Alaska to this trip to Alaska? Actually this trip is a part of the training that I have planned for her. She will be attending four more seminars this year, by the end of which, Alaska will be able to present spiritual seminars on her own. These are practical training trips and as such, I will be grateful if you do not insist on paying for them."

Maxim paused and listened to Alaska's father for a few seconds. Then he said "Thank you Mr. Ashley. Would you like to have a word with Alaska?"

Maxim gave the phone back to Alaska. Her father said "Gladiator makes it very difficult to contradict him. Learn all you can from him. You are privileged. He is actually giving you one-to-one coaching, which I don't think he has ever done. Telephone before you leave for Anchorage. And thank Gladiator and take care little one."

Alaska and Maxim arrived at the resort in Denali at 4 PM. They had stopped for couple of minutes for a snack on way to the resort. The seminar was scheduled to start at 5 PM. They checked in in the resort and met the organizer, who was very relieved to see them. He said "There are 250 people in this group, all above sixty years. They are eagerly waiting for the seminar to begin. Mr. De Winter, I do hope you can answer all their questions and satisfy them. I should warn you that it is nearly impossible to satisfy them."

Maxim smiled but didn't comment. They straight went to their rooms to change. Maxim had requested Alaska not to wear jeans for the seminars. So, she had brought a long black wrap-around skirt with one big red rose embroidered in the front. She wore it with a white lace collared blouse and a red cardigan. When she came out of her room, she found Maxim in suit and tie, waiting for her.

He smiled and murmured "Absolutely enchanting!"

The organizer, who was waiting for them in the lobby, took them to the auditorium. Alaska was surprised to see the hall packed although they still had 15 minutes to go. Maxim asked the organizer to place another chair and a table on the stage. He then walked out of the hall along with Alaska. When they were out he said "Sit on the stage with me, not with the audience, not tonight. Take notes or write your comments about my presentation. I saw a lot of pads and pencils at the entrance door."

Alaska looked at Maxim and asked "Why?"

Maxim softly said "I want you where I can see you, Princess! Do you want some tea or coffee?"

Alaska shook her head. She turned to look outside through big glass windows and said "Oh, Maxim, the clouds have parted! You can see the snow covered Mt. Kinley range. It is beautiful! Look, Maxim, look!"

Maxim agreed "Yes, very beautiful." But when Alaska looked at him, she found his Indigo eyes unwaveringly fixed on her.

She said "Hey Maxim, you are not even looking at Mt. Kinley!"

Maxim laughed and said "I saw what I wanted to see! Let us go in. Be with me all the time. Sense the vibration of the audience, especially at the beginning and at the close of the seminar."

They walked in and went up the stage. Alaska sat on a chair with a note pad and pencil in her hands.

Maxim walked to the center of the stage with his usual smile and looked piercingly at the audience. Alaska knew he was reading the vibration of the audience.

Then, he began "Good evening my friends. An invitation from your group was indeed a welcome surprise! I do feel honored for being asked to talk in the presence of such an elite group."

As he paused, an old lady who was sitting in the front row, with a mike, asked "Our group has been asking you to come for more than a year but you didn't bother to come. Why? Was it because we are not young and you didn't want to waste your time with us? I hear you like to teach only young people. Is that true?"

Maxim smiled and said "No, not true."

"What do you mean 'not true'? Why didn't you accept our invitation earlier?" she almost barked.

"Because, you did not want me to come or even expect me to come as much as the other group did and even now you were doubting if I would come!" gently replied Maxim.

"What? What other group?" she asked sounding very annoyed.

"You see, in a year, I can present only so many seminars and people at my spiritual school decide which ones I present personally. My friend, do you know what influences them to choose some and reject some? It is the power of attraction of the group inviting me. So, if I didn't come here last year, it was because other groups inviting me were more passionate, more desirous of my presence."

Maxim paused giving time to the lady to digest this information.

Then he continued "My presence here, even today, is not caused by the power of attraction of your group! I have broken some rules to be here today because it was in Alaska, where my friend, Alaska, deigned/condescended to grace Earth with her heavenly presence!"

Maxim waited for the reaction to his words.

After a short silence, an old gentleman, slightly mystified, asked "Is there somebody called Alaska?"

In answer Maxim turned towards Alaska and slightly bowed to her. Alaska was feeling uncomfortable. She almost asked out loud "what are you doing Maxim?" Then she saw him, his eyes twinkling, he was trying not to laugh. He was having fun talking with these complaining senior citizens, may be, he wanted them to realize, the more they complain, the more things they will have to complain about!

Then another senior lady joined in the dialogue. She asked "You love this heavenly Alaska who condescended to come to Earth?"

Maxim responded immediately "But, of course! Who wouldn't?" he said with a big smile.

Alaska didn't like this conversation one bit and shook her head in disapproval, when she was further surprised to hear the first lady say in a critical tone to her "Why do you shake your head like that? I would have given anything to hear a man declare his love for me, in presence of hundreds of people!"

Alaska glared at Maxim who was openly laughing now. Half the audience had joined him, some were even clapping.

When he could stop laughing, he said "I think I have answered all your questions, so, we can wrap up the seminar now."

"What? Wrap up the seminar? We have not even started." said the first lady indignantly.

Maxim smiled and said "In that case, I suggest, start now. We don't have much time as I have a dinner engagement tonight."

"What is the answer to the question 'who am I?' asked the lady.

"Close your eyes and ask yourself for the answer" replied Maxim.

"But I never get any answer!" retorted the lady.

"After asking the question, do you wait for the answer?" asked Maxim.

"How long do I have to wait?" asked the lady.

"For as long as it takes!" was the prompt reply from Maxim.

"What do you mean?" she asked impatiently.

"I mean, if your question was important and your life depended on the answer, won't you wait till you get the answer?" asked Maxim.

After a short pause, Maxim continued "So, the first thing to ask yourself is, is the question, and its answer, important to you? Is it worth the trouble? What is the benefit? Do you even think there is any possibility of someone answering you? Do you even think it is possible for you to be anything but this physical body?"

Maxim silently watched the lady who had complained that she never got any answer.

After thinking for some time, the lady said "I don't know. I really don't know. I don't understand. Gladiator, won't you teach all this today?"

Maxim smiled and gently replied "It would have been my pleasure except I am not a professional teacher. Please contact my spiritual school. Every imaginable information is available there, besides, the best spiritual teachers are there to help you, should you need any personal help. I only want to awaken a desire in every heart to know who or what they are, and to know their own powers to create and live the life of their dreams."

After a short pause he continued "Anyway, let me answer your first question 'who am I?' for you. In short, you are not your body. You are limitless empty Space, boundless Awareness with power beyond the comprehension of your mind. My friends know that you are creating your reality by your thoughts, feelings and beliefs. No use blaming others for the way your life is turning out to be, because it is you, and only you, that is creating your circumstances leading to your present life. If you do not like your present situation, simply change your thoughts and beliefs, and thus change your life. It is entirely your choice!"

Someone from the back of the hall shouted "NO, that is not true. That is a lie!"

Maxim stopped. He saw the boy Allen, from the airport whom they had encouraged to come to his seminar, standing there waving his hands to draw his attention.

Maxim smiled and said "Could you please give him a mike so that we can hear his objections and may be, help him?"

Everyone turned to look at him. One old gentleman said "We don't know him. He is not from our group."

Maxim softly said "His question and/or objection may be of use to others too. Who knows?"

When the mike reached him, Allen vehemently said "I don't believe you. If, what you preach, is true, then change me – make me look like you, make me a billionaire like you and make that girl run to me as she had run to you at the airport!"

Maxim smiled and said "You are missing the point, my friend. I cannot change you but you can change yourself because you are the Source Creator of your reality. As I said, if you don't like your present life, then change it by changing your thoughts, beliefs, and your self-image! Never envy anyone, never copy anyone. You are born with your unique un-paralleled talents. Tell me, would you really like to stand here and ask people to get acquainted with their True-self, as I do? Would you really like to travel around the world, to successfully conduct business to make millions for the needy, for the children who need food and education urgently, as I do?"

Maxim continued "As for Alaska, you will be out of your depth if she did come to you. Spirituality is her passion and that is what she is going to teach. Do you understand the subject? Does it interest you? I don't think so my friend. I don't think so."

After a short pause he continued "But let us presume that your dream is to become such an irresistibly attractive man that girls come running to you at airports. Well, if that is your dream, then the answer is 'YES', it is possible, you can become a man like that. But remember only you can create this new man. No one else can do it for you."

After another pause Maxim said "Yes, I can sense your question. You want to know 'how'. The answer is simple – change yourself! You want to be different, you have to become different. How- by changing yourself! You cannot keep doing the same old things and expect to get different results. So, start by changing your habits, your beliefs, your actions, your environment, your company etc. This is the first step."

"The second step is to get acquainted with your True-self, your inner magician, as I call it, so that you realize your own power, the power to create the life of your dreams."

"The third step is to meditate, meditate to silence your analytical mind so that you can bring coherence between your mind and heart. Now visualize with feeling, the man you want to become. Feel you already are that man. As soon as you can feel and believe it, you are transformed. You can do it if you choose to do it. It is your choice as I was saying earlier. Contact my spiritual school. They will help you at every step, for free. Believe me, you are more powerful than you can imagine."

Maxim stopped and asked Alaska "Would you like to say something that may help our friend here?"

Alaska picked up the mike from the table and said "Allen, you must find your passion first. If you are not sure, watch yourself. What you are curious about. What gives you joy? Follow your little 'joys'. It will lead you to the big one – your true desire, your dream. Ignite your passion Allen, ignite it! It will transform you."

Maxim was looking at Alaska with a gentle smile.

Alaska continued "I am telling you all this from my personal experience. When I heard Gladiator for the first time, I didn't believe him. I too didn't know my passion, but once I knew it I followed it with joy and excitement, and the result was that I started to see glimpses of my True-self, the inner magician, and when that happened, for the first time in my life I experienced bliss, an un-deniable joy, of feeling cherished, celebrated and loved. I was at absolute peace within myself."

Alaska paused for a second, then continued "Allen, don't waste your days drifting from place to place aimlessly. Find your dream and then create the life of your dreams! You have the power to create anything you can ever imagine. Do it! You will not regret it!"

Maxim, who had been watching Alaska, said to her with a smile "You did hit the nail on the head. Thank you Princess."

Maxim looked at the audience and asked "Any questions?"

A lady from the second row raised her hand. When she got the mike she said "I come for your seminars just to listen to you Gladiator. I know from my personal experience that whatever you say, whenever you say and where ever you say, is always the most appropriate for the moment. Asking questions is a waste of time, I think, because you know better than we do what we need to know at this moment in time."

A lot of people clapped to show their appreciation of what she had said.

The lady continued "So, Gladiator, please say something that you think we need to hear now, say something that will make us aware of our True-self."

Maxim smiled and said "Thank you for your kind words, my friend. Please give me a moment."

There was complete silence in the auditorium. Alaska knew Maxim was reading the vibration of the audience.

After a few seconds He began "Most of you, my friends, are aware of the fact that you are spiritual beings with no limitations and with un-imaginable powers to create a reality of your choice. Am I right?"

Maxim looked at his audience and heard 'yes' from them.

He asked "But do you believe it? The day you believe it, acknowledge it, own it, you become the ultimate magician that you were born to be. You take your rightful place as creators in this divine universe. My friends, the real power is in the knowledge of your True-self. I encourage you to bring your True-self from being just a concept to being absolutely real in your daily life. I want you to feel the joy, the love, the freedom that will be yours when you live in complete awareness of your True-self. I keep repeating this to awaken a desire in your hearts to know your True-self. Awaken yourselves, my magicians! Once you know your power, you will be free!"

Alaska smiled as, as always, there was silence after Maxim stopped speaking, as if the audience was hoping to hear something more.

After a few seconds Maxim said with a smile "Let us go and see what food we have created for dinner tonight. Whatever you did create, enjoy it my friends. Bon Appetite!"

Saying this, Maxim, along with Alaska, started moving out of the hall. Pandemonium broke out. The hall erupted to life. The audience surrounded them with endless questions.

Maxim, with his gentle smile said "Answers to all your questions are at my website. I encourage you to connect with it. Please excuse us, as we have a dinner engagement. We have to go now. Good night my magicians. I hope, the magic of this beautiful place will add to your own creative powers to create a world of your dreams."

Maxim softly said to Alaska "Go to your room. Pick up your jacket and scarf and wait for me there."

As Alaska made to move she saw Allen standing right in front of her. Allen said "Sorry for being rude. Forgive me Alaska." Then he looked at Maxim and said "Please forgive me. I was angry. I was angry with myself for being the way I am. I want to be like you Gladiator. I want to become a person with whom Alaska would like to talk. Help me. Gladiator, help me. Please!"

Maxim's brilliant Indigo eyes were fixed on Allen. Allen became silent under Maxim's piercing look. After a few seconds, Maxim said "Allen, close your eyes. Now, take a slow deep breath. Take two more very slow deep breaths. OK, now open your eyes. Allen, your desire to change has already transformed you in the non-physical realm. Your limiting beliefs are dropping off you. Let them go! Now, Allen, it is time for you to 'dream', find out your true passion and follow it. Yes, my ultimate magician, you can do it!"

Saying this Maxim again asked Alaska to go and turned towards the crowd still waiting to talk with him.

Alaska quickly went to her room, took her jacket and scarf out and waited for Maxim to come. She looked at the clock. It was nearly ten minutes since she came to her room. She went out of her room to check what was keeping him. She was debating whether to go to the lobby to check, when she saw him coming. He quickly telephoned their driver to get the car immediately for them, and then, he went inside his room, took off his tie and jacket, pulled on a thick sweater, picked up his over-coat and said with a grin "Let us go before anyone catches us."

As they reached the lobby, several people asked Maxim the time for the morning meditation. Without stopping Maxim confirmed "Yes, we meet at 5.30 AM."

Alaska was surprised to hear it. She didn't know that they will have a meditation class too. Maxim guided her to the waiting car and soon they were off. He asked the driver to drive them to the restaurant he had seen on way to the resort.

Maxim looked at Alaska and said "It is great to have you here with me."

Alaska smiled and asked him "Are you conducting a morning meditation for the 'senior citizens'?"

"Yes. They wanted to ask questions and have endless discussions on spirituality, which is a waste of time. Fifteen minutes of meditation with us will raise their vibration so much that they are bound to feel better and be more focused on their spiritual path. What do you think?"

Alaska replied "Yes, that is true. It is your presence. It is the energy that you radiate 24/7 that raises our vibration. Maxim, if you wanted to give more time to them, we could have had dinner at the Resort itself."

Maxim smiled and replied "Yes, we could have, but there was a problem. I wanted to have dinner with you and you alone Princess! Don't you know that?"

Alaska could hear her heart thud at this, but she didn't know how to respond, so she smiled but kept quiet.

Soon they were at the restaurant. It was quite big and well lighted. Obviously they didn't believe in the romantic dinners with dimmed lights. It was nearly full but they did find a table. Maxim asked Alaska "Would you like to have the famous Alaskan Salmon or would you prefer something else?"

"I will have the Salmon." replied Alaska.

After ordering the food Maxim asked Alaska "So, let us hear your comments on today's seminar."

Alaska thoughtfully said "It was different, wasn't it? People were in a critical mood. I wonder why."

Maxim replied "When people attend spiritual seminars just because it is something to do, or it is a done thing or it is a fashionable thing to do, without true desire, they criticize for the sake of appearing knowledgeable and/or to engage in an intellectual discussion. My mission is to awaken true desire for spiritual knowledge, knowledge that will bring un-imaginable benefits to one and all. I asked the lady to go to my website because I wanted her to make some effort for acquiring this sacred knowledge. It will make her appreciate the knowledge more."

When Maxim paused, Alaska asked "Why did you ask me to speak today?"

Maxim replied "There were two reasons for it. The obvious one was, of course, Allen. He was angry and frustrated because he felt rejected by you. He wanted to hit out at you through me. So, when you spoke directly to him, the power of your rejection got mitigated and he became receptive to our suggestions. I am sure, your authentic tale of your experience with the love of your True-self, has touched him deep. You succeeded in changing him, changing him for a better and happier version of himself. Congratulations beautiful Princess!"

Maxim paused to tuck a strand of hair behind her ear and continued "The second reason. When I asked you to speak, did you notice you didn't hesitate even for a second? You picked up the mike and started speaking because you wanted to help Allen. You didn't feel nervous, you didn't think whether you should or you should not, the thought upper most in your mind was to HELP him. That is what you will always do. Just have a genuine desire to help and you have the recipe for a successful seminar. Princess, whether you know it or not, you are ready to present spiritual seminars!"

Alaska was looking confused. She asked with doubt written on her face "Am I Maxim?"

Maxim laughed and said "Yes, you are. Forget it. Let us enjoy the food. I can see some French-fries still on your plate. Finish it off then we will order some dessert."

****

It was extremely cold when Alaska and Maxim returned from their dinner to the Resort. Alaska ran inside the hotel and Maxim followed her in. Alaska saw a big fire blazing in the fire place at the back of the lobby. She ran to it and spread her hands to warm them. She could smell coffee. She looked around. On the right side of the fire place, she saw a table loaded with tea and coffee things. Alaska asked Maxim if he would like some coffee as she was going to pour a cup for herself.

"Sure." Replied Maxim and moved towards the sofa near the fire place.

Alaska, when she returned to the fire place, was surprised to see Maxim softly strumming a guitar. She placed his coffee on the table near him and asked if he could play guitar. She had seen a boy playing it when they had arrived at the Resort. Maxim nodded and kept humming a tune accompanied by the guitar. It sounded so good. Alaska exclaimed "Oh, Maxim, I didn't know you could sing and play guitar so well."

Maxim smiled and said "A gift from my father, I suppose. Martin used to say about my father-'there wasn't a song he couldn't sing, there wasn't an instrument he couldn't play and there wasn't a beat he couldn't dance to!"

"Wow! Really? I loved the tune you were just playing. Please play again." said Alaska.

Maxim looked at her and said with a smile "Your wish is my command, Princess." He began playing the guitar while singing very softly "You have enchanted me, you have captivated me, you have imprisoned me…"

Alaska said "Oh"

He continued humming and playing the guitar with a teasing smile "still life is beautiful because you are in it…"

Alaska again said "Oh" She knew she was blushing, although she was not sure why. To cover her confusion, she said flippantly "Maxim, are you trying to flirt with me?"

Maxim kept playing the guitar and answered "I never 'try' to do anything. I do them."

Alaska said "Oh, well, then, are you flirting with me?"

Maxim put the guitar on the table, picked up his cup of coffee and replied slowly "No."

Alaska asked "No?"

Maxim thoughtfully replied "What is flirting, Princess? I think it is to act or behave as if one is attracted to someone, only for the sake of amusement. It is not genuine. Well, that does not describe me for sure."

After few seconds he continued "If you must have a word or a phrase to describe or label my action, the nearest phrase would be 'making love'."

Alaska's eyes were round with surprise. She could only say "Oh."

Maxim smiled and asked "Confused you, have I?"

After a few moments he said "The phrase 'making love' has a general connotation of, shall we say, lust or inflamed physical passion, but it need not be that, not necessarily, not always. It depends on the meaning you have given to the word 'love'. If you believe it is totally a physical feeling that you feel for someone out there, then it is a short physical experience. In the absence of love, that is, true love, the non-physical love, this physical attraction usually withers away just as a plant withers away in the absence of water."

Maxim stopped for a second and took Alaska's hand in his and said "Love is the most magnificent emotional vibration that humans can experience. It is within you, and you radiate it to others without any condition or expectation. This feeling of 'making love' endures and cannot wither away. Actually the romance of the non-physical is of un-paralleled beauty."

Alaska was spellbound.

Maxim gently said "To answer your question again, no, Princess, I never flirt with you."

Maxim got up and said "It is getting late. Let us go. I have to catch up with Enterprise work before I sleep. Morning meditation is at 5.30 AM. Be there. Together we will raise the vibration of the senior citizens so that they feel happier than they have felt for quite some time."

CHAPTER 7

Alaska was walking back from her class in the evening deep in thought with a smile playing on her lips. She was remembering her trip to Alaska last month with Maxim. Whenever Maxim was around, everything looked brighter, more colorful, as if the world had awakened from a long hibernation. Her logical mind told her it was Maxim's high vibration that made everything more vibrant, but she wondered, was it? Anyway, she had to concede that every time she met him she learned something new. She was so engrossed in her thoughts that she didn't hear or see the man calling her from across the road. She was startled when the man touched her arm and said "Alaska?"

Alaska looked up and saw Mark smiling at her. She was pleasantly surprised to see him and said with a smile "Hi Mark, when did you come? It is great to see you after such a long time."

Mark smiled and said "You are as beautiful as ever Aly. Let us go to our cafeteria and have coffee. Shall we?"

Alaska nodded and started walking towards the cafeteria.

They found a table for two. Alaska sat down while Mark went to get the coffee. When Mark was back with their coffee Alaska asked "What are you doing here? I miss you Mark, you, Julie and James. We used to have so much fun together."

Mark replied softly "It is as well you don't know how much I have missed you Alaska." After a moment he continued "A girl at my office had to come here. Her mother was admitted to a hospital today and I offered to drive her here. I will be going back tonight."

Alaska asked "Do you enjoy your work?"

Mark replied "It is ok, but I have decided to quit it and do the Masters beginning this September. How about you? Enjoying yourself?"

Alaska replied "Yes. Life is great and I am enjoying my classes."

Mark asked "Still practicing Gladiator's meditation etc.?"

Alaska said with a big smile "Oh, yes. I love it."

After a moment Mark asked "Have you seen him recently?"

Alaska asked "Who? Maxim? Yes. Whenever he comes to Boston I see him and every time I learn something new. Actually I have attended two of his seminars recently. The last one was in Alaska."

Mark looked surprised. He asked "You go out of town to attend his seminars? Have you started working for him? Do you get paid?"

Alaska replied "Of course not. Why should he pay me? I am learning how to present spiritual seminars as Maxim does. I am going to attend six of his seminars this year. He said for the first five, I will listen to him and the last one I will present and he will listen."

Mark said "Really? I cannot believe it. You must have progressed hell of a lot on the spiritual path if Gladiator thinks you can present a seminar."

Alaska smiled and said "I don't know Mark."

After a moment Mark said "Yes, I think you have Aly. I can almost feel your high vibration. I can feel the electric tingle go through me when you look unwaveringly like Gladiator does."

Just then her phone rang. She was surprised to see it was from Maxim who was somewhere out of country.

Happily she said "Hi Maxim, where are you?"

"Some 5000 miles away from you." said Maxim. He continued "I have been invited by a group of successful entrepreneurs to present a seminar for them on board a cruise in the Caribbean. They have been asking for quite some time but my school could not accommodate them in my schedule. This group, they say, has done all my basic courses, and now, want to make quantum leap on their spiritual path. It would be different but interesting too. Would you like to come, Princess?"

"Oh, wow, I would love to come but I have my exams coming up." replied Alaska.

"It will be fixed for a week end so that you don't miss anything important. OK? Then I will accept it."

"Oh yes, please!" replied Alaska all excited.

Suddenly Maxim asked "You are not alone, are you? Where are you?"

"At the cafeteria" replied Alaska.

"With whom? With Mark?" asked Maxim.

"Why do you even ask when you know everything." Alaska retorted.

Maxim gently replied "No, I don't know everything. I only know things that concern you, Princess. How is Mark?"

Alaska replied "He is fine."

Maxim surprised her by asking "Would he like to speak with me?"

Alaska asked Mark "Would you like to speak with Maxim?"

Mark was astonished. He said "What? Gladiator wants to speak with me? Are you sure?"

Alaska nodded and passed her phone to him.

Mark formally said "Good evening. It is very kind of you to…."

Maxim interrupted him and said "How are you Mark? How has life been? Has someone walked in in your arms and your heart?"

Mark was surprised at the question and remained silent for some time, then replied "Yes, someone has, but my heart does not accept. It prefers to remain with the memory of the love that was, is and will be my love for ever."

Maxim gently said "That is your choice Mark. But I hope you will remember the love that you feel is within you, not in her. She is a trigger for you to connect with the stream of Divine love. This physical 3D world is quite confusing my friend. It appears to be so solid, so real, that it makes you forget that it is only a make-believe game that you are playing. You get so attached to the characters in your game that it breaks your heart if you lose them. Mark, I have gone through it and I also chose to wait for my love, life after life, for thousands of years. So, I understand and appreciate your decision. But never forget, you are the ultimate magician. Never look for others to make you happy, they never will, not because they don't want to, but because they cannot! Only you have the power to choose to feel happy and loved, and then feel it. The bliss of love is within you, not out there! Mark, you were born extra-ordinary. Don't try to live an ordinary life."

There was a long silence on the line. At last Mark spoke "I know I am privileged to have known you Gladiator and to have spoken with you today. You always make me see things differently. You create a new perspective of the world for me. And you do energize me even from thousands of miles away. I don't know where you are but accept my thanks, my gratitude for what you do. Thank you." Saying this he gave the phone back to Alaska without a word.

Alaska took the phone and asked Maxim "What did you say? Mark is deeply moved."

Maxim replied "Be gentle with your friend, Princess. And, What I said to Mark? Well, read me, you will know it. OK, why don't you read me now and tell me what I am thinking."

Alaska closed her eyes and focused all her attention on Maxim. After a moment she asked "Lacking? Missing?"

Maxim said "Yes, you are right, but who is missing whom?"

When Alaska kept silent, Maxim laughed and said "I understand your dilemma. You are right, I am missing you. I am missing your beautiful smile, your twinkling eyes, just about everything Princess. Do you know you have the dubious honor of being the only person to make me forget that we are spiritual beings playing a game in this 3D world? You got me so immersed in the game that I was going to bi-locate and be physically with you. It is as well I didn't. I wonder who would have been more surprised, I or Mark?"

When Alaska didn't respond, Maxim asked "How are things with Jacque? Dazzled by your smile yet or still staring at you?"

Alaska replied "He is still the same. He makes me feel sad and uncomfortable. I don't know why."

Maxim said "Hmm, don't worry too much. For your information I am in France and as the French would say 'Bonne nuit ma cherie'."

Alaska responded "Bonne nuit ma….."

Maxim corrected her "You say 'bonne nuit mon cher'."

Alaska repeated it and then asked "What does cher exactly mean?"

Maxim laughed and said, before disconnecting the phone "Don't worry you said the right thing to the right man, Princess."

Alaska was aware Mark had been watching her. She didn't know what to say to Mark when he asked "You love him, don't you?"

Alaska thought for a moment. She replied "I don't know. Love is the most splendored thing in our creation. I wonder if I am capable of it Mark."

Mark smiled and said "Well, I better go now. Ruth must be waiting for me. It was great meeting you again Alaska. I am going to come more often to meet you and meet Gladiator too. Where ever you are, I know, he will be there. I will have the privilege of meeting both of you at the same time. Gladiator is amazing, isn't he?"

Alaska replied "Yes, he is. Mark, we are physically focused, and we rarely focus on our True-self, while Maxim is totally focused on, aware of and one with the True-self. He is actually more divine than most of us. That is the difference. He is always thinking of ways to help others. Always!"

Mark got up and said "Do let me know when you will be presenting your first seminar. I cannot wait to hear it. And could you inform me when Gladiator would be coming here next?"

Alaska said "Oh, I forgot to tell you, Maxim has said he will come here for a day so that he can meet you, Julie and James. I will let you know the date."

Mark asked "How does he remember our names? You told him?"

Alaska replied "I don't think so, at least not recently. He always enquires about you three and my parents. He is an extremely kind person Mark."

Mark nodded and said "Yes, that is true. Take care of yourself. You are precious, Aly, very precious to more than one person."

CHAPTER 8

Alaska was all excited about the seminar on board the Caribbean cruise. Maxim had told her that it was a five day cruise starting from Miami, but as they could not spare 5 days, they will fly to San Juan and join the cruise there for only two nights.

And now Alaska was on board the flight to San Juan with Maxim. Even now she could hardly believe she was actually traveling with Maxim to attend one of his seminars. She used to dream about it and here, she was doing just that. Anything she desired, and didn't doubt, came to pass. She felt grateful and now she understood what Maxim meant when he said 'your desire gets fulfilled just by desiring them'.

Alaska peeped up to see what Maxim was doing and was met by a quizzical look in his Indigo eyes.

He said "Take a nap for an hour or two. Your father said you didn't sleep last night, kept chatting with your mother."

Alaska replied in a worried voice "Maxim, why does my mother worry so much about my safety? I am grown up but she cannot stop telling me how to behave with people. She even told me how I should behave with you, respect you as a teacher, as a Guru, and keep my distance and not take your kindness for granted etc.!"

Maxim looked at her and said "Princess, sometime next month I am going to come and spend a day with your parents."

Alaska was surprised to hear it. She asked "Why? Why do you want to spend a day with my parents?"

Maxim smiled and said "Once they know me, they will stop worrying about your safety."

Alaska grumbled "I wonder. I told Mom with you around, I feel absolutely safe, but that didn't satisfy her."

Maxim gently said "I think I understand her. I must meet her soon to put her mind at rest. Alright, close your eyes and sleep. We have a long evening ahead of us Princess."

Alaska closed her eyes but kept thinking about her parents. When she had asked her father for her passport, which was needed for the cruise, her father had sounded a little doubtful. He had asked her if she would be alright on the cruise with Maxim. Alaska thought that they worried because they didn't know Maxim as she did. He was kind, caring and over-protective.

Later her mother had called her and said that they will be coming to Boston to hand over her passport and to see her off. Yesterday they had arrived and she had enjoyed having dinner with them. Alaska had moved to their hotel from her dorm and had chatted with her mother till the wee hours in the morning. Dorothy had sent her air ticket. Maxim was to meet her at the airport. He had said if by any chance he missed the flight to San Juan from Boston, Alaska should go ahead and he will meet her at San Juan airport.

Alaska, with her parents, had arrived early at the airport for her flight. Alaska looked around but could not see Maxim anywhere. She checked in her small suitcase and asked the girl at the counter if Maxim had checked in. Her heart sank when the girl said 'no, he hadn't. She closed her eyes and fervently said "Maxim, please, please come."

When she came out, her mother had asked "You are traveling in Business class?" Alaska nodded her head without saying anything. And then she had seen Maxim waving at her. She was thrilled to see him and as usual had started to run, but then remembered her parents and had stopped. She waved back. Her parents had been relieved and happy to see him. After checking his bag, he had said "We have enough time for a cup of tea or coffee before our flight."

Maxim had asked her mother "Would you like a cup of tea, Mrs. Ashley?"

Alaska had wanted to say 'no', but her mother had accepted his offer saying "If you are sure you have enough time, then, yes, I would like some tea."

Maxim found a café and ordered tea for them. Alaska had said she didn't want anything. She was feeling disappointed. Maxim had not said a word to her since he came. His complete attention was on her parents.

Just then she had heard "Look up Princess!" She had looked at Maxim, and he had smiled while waiting for the tea at the counter.

Maxim had continued silently "You haven't said a word to me either, have you? And I am waiting for my welcome hug!"

Alaska had almost laughed out loud at that.

Maxim had come back with a tray loaded with four cups. He gave the tea to her parents, and then asked Alaska "Could you please get the plate of scones from the counter?"

Alaska had said "Oh, sorry" and had run to get the plate.

What Alaska didn't know was that Maxim had deliberately sent her to get the scones so that he could talk to her parents. The moment Alaska left, Maxim asked her mother "Mrs. Ashley, something is worrying you. Can I help?"

Alaska's father had immediately said "Annie, this is your chance. Ask Gladiator and then, you can relax."

Alaska's mother had said "Alaska is still a child at heart. I worry about her. She is simple and straight forward but the world is not like that Gladiator!"

Maxim had replied "Please don't worry any more. I won't let anything or anybody hurt her in anyway, ever!"

Maxim had looked at Alaska who was walking back with the plate of scones. He had continued "She looks like a fragile angel but I assure you she is a sovereign goddess. Darkness, in any form, cannot remain in her presence!"

Alaska had reached their table. With a smile she had told her mother "Mom. Try the scone. It is freshly baked. It smells so good!"

Maxim had pushed a cup of coffee towards her saying "this is for you."

Alaska had said "Hey, I didn't ask for coffee, did I?"

Maxim had said with a smile "No, you didn't. But I got it for you because you will like it with the hot scones. Quickly eat up we don't have much time, Princess."

He had asked for her passport. He had checked it and kept in his pocket to complete forms for the Cruise.

After getting final instructions from her mother to be careful she had left with Maxim for the flight.

So, that was that.

Alaska opened her eyes to see if Maxim was awake. His eyes were closed, so she adjusted the little pillow and closed her eyes and slept.

****

Alaska, with Maxim, had just boarded the cruise ship. The main lobby was huge and beautiful teaming with people from all around the world. The live music made Alaska want to dance. She smiled and thought this ship was like a busy town. People were coming and going with children running and laughing around the lobby. Yes, she thought, the ship was vibrant with life.

After checking in Maxim asked Alaska "What do you want to do now? Want to eat something? Or would you like to explore the ship? I think it is a good time to explore because most of the passengers, who have gone ashore to San Juan, the second stopover of the cruise, aren't back. The ship should be fairly empty."

Alaska excitedly said "Let us explore the ship first!"

They checked a detailed map of the ship. Each floor of the ship had something different. Alaska had fun checking out the pools, the roller-coasters, the library, the restaurants and the decks. When she got tired walking from the stern to the front of the ship on each floor, she stood looking through the huge glass window at the bow of the ship.

Suddenly she asked Maxim "Can we go to the front deck and stand at the bow like a figurehead on old boats?"

Maxim laughed and said "No, you cannot become a figurehead of the ship but yes, we can go to the bow and stand at the front most part of the ship. I don't see anyone there, so let us go now."

They quickly went down and out on the deck. No one was there. Alaska stood at the front most point of the ship. She had not noticed earlier that the ship had started moving. The breeze was quite strong and she could feel the swaying movement of the ship which she was not aware of, inside the ship. She shivered and grabbed the front railing to steady herself. Maxim came and stood right behind her with his arms encircling her holding the railings on both sides.

Alaska asked him "You won't let me fall?"

Maxim replied "No, I won't."

Alaska relaxed, let go of the railings and leaned back against him. She closed her eyes. She felt as if she was riding the ocean waves or was she soaring high in the quantum field of all possibilities? She stood like that for a few minutes relishing the feel of total freedom when she became aware of voices. Voices? She opened her eyes and was surprised to see people around them.

She said to Maxim "Let us go."

There was no reaction from him. He stood behind her with his arms on both sides holding her in place. Alaska twisted to look at Maxim and realized he was silently laughing.

She asked "Why are you laughing? Let us go. There are too many people here."

When Maxim could speak, he said "Oh, Princess, you have crushed my ego into smithereens! Here I was thinking you would only be aware of me and my arms around you, but obviously other people take precedence."

Alaska laughed and retorted "No, they don't, but it is your fault. Where ever you go you attract people like a magnet!"

Maxim laughed and walked towards the door, saying Hi and good evening, to the people who had suddenly appeared on the deck.

When they were inside, Maxim said with a big grin "Princess, believe me, you will always set the decks on fire, where ever you go. Why – because, you are vibrating at a high frequency, at a very high frequency compared to other people. You may not be aware of it but that is the reason why people get attracted to you. Use your power of attraction to help people become aware of their own inherent powers."

Maxim smiled and said "Ok, enough of that. Where do we go now? Let us eat something before we start the seminar otherwise you will be thinking of food instead of the audience. I have a feeling it is going to be a long evening. So, where do you want to go? Name the place."

Alaska said "Let us go to the 'Blue Lagoon'. I liked the décor of the restaurant."

Maxim said with a grin and a bow "Blue Lagoon? Your wish is my command. Let us go."

Alaska looked at him. Maxim looked so different in a T-shirt and laughing in this care-free way. No one would believe that he was Gladiator, the world famous spiritual teacher whose mission was to awaken humanity to their own inherent power to create a world of their dreams, full of harmony and love.

****

Ten minutes before the seminar, Maxim and Alaska were on way to the auditorium. Maxim, in black suit with white silk shirt and tie, looked impressive and attractive no wonder people could not take their eyes off him, thought Alaska. She had changed into a long turquoise green dress with an Indigo- purple scarf around her neck. When she had come out of her room, Maxim was waiting for her. He silently looked at her from head to toe and murmured "Absolutely breathtaking! You better be with me on the stage this evening."

The auditorium was, as usual, full when they reached it. As they went up the stage, the audience became silent, and as they turned to face them someone asked surprised "Is he the spiritual teacher?' followed by "oh" "wow".

Without replying Maxim asked the attendant to get another chair, and a mike for them. After fixing his own mike, he waved to the audience with his usual smile. Alaska's full attention was on the audience. She was getting mixed vibe from the audience. She noted it down without being aware of the curious and admiring glances of the audience.

Then Maxim began "No, I am not a spiritual teacher, neither is she! I am here to awaken a desire, a curiosity in your hearts to know who you truly are! You can use your immense power to create your desired world, only if, you knew who or what you are! Isn't it so?"

After a little pause he turned towards Alaska and said with a smile "I call her Princess, because she is a princess, but her parents prefer to call her Alaska, because that is the sacred place on planet Earth where she chose to grace us with her enchanting presence and to captivate us for the rest of our lives!"

Alaska was so surprised to hear it that she laughed out loud. Everyone laughed. Alaska realized, soon, everyone's attention was totally on her.

She said with a smile "Good evening, Gladiator's ultimate magicians!"

There was a chorus of 'good evenings'.

Maxim continued "Don't get bewitched by her smile! Be careful. She is reading you like an open book!"

"What?" was the response from the audience.

Maxim was enjoying their reactions. He laughed and said "I was informed that you are a group of successful entrepreneurs, which means, you are dreamers. You know your dreams, you know you are the creators and you already are consciously creating your dreams.

You, obviously, follow the advice of your True-self, through your intuition and ESP, in your business dealings. You asked for this seminar, I believe, hoping to make quantum leaps. My friends, quantum leaps into what? Do you want to know our final frontier? Love! Yes, it is love. Love is the essential nature of our Creator. Love is the sacred spiritual force of creation. You can say love is the cosmic glue that keeps our ever expanding universe together."

Maxim stopped and looked keenly at his audience. There was silence, may be, everyone was trying to understand this love.

He continued "You are an individualized aspect of the Creator and you are made out of the same god stuff. So, love is your essence as well! If you want to make quantum leaps in your evolution, you need to be constantly aware of this divine stream of love. Meditate till you awaken your consciousness and be one with it. Become one with this no-thing, the empty space, the awareness, the ever loving witness!"

Maxim paused for a few moments, then, asked "Is that what you wanted to do?"

When there was no response to his question, Maxim said "Ah, I get it. You want to know if connecting with this divine stream of love will help you to make quantum leaps into future successes in the 3D world. Am I right?"

"Yes, please" was the answer.

Maxim asked "You already know the formula for manifesting your desire."

Spontaneous answer was "Dream, then follow your dream, and then live the life of your dreams!"

Maxim laughed and said "Good. When you are consciously connected with your true-self, when you become one with the non-physical 'no-thing', the loving silent witness that you are, you skip the second step of the process. You won't need the second step of 'follow your dream' because your True-self has no doubts, no limiting beliefs what-so-ever! Your manifestation can almost be instantaneous, if you so desired!"

Maxim stopped and looked at Alaska who was sitting there. Alaska gave him a thumbs-up sign with a big smile. Maxim bowed to her and turned towards the audience. There was visible excitement in the crowd.

Maxim asked "So, my magicians how will you do it? Usually you are not aware of your True-self, are you?"

"Please, Gladiator, won't you tell us the best and the easiest way to be one with our True-self? Please!" a lady pleaded from the very back of the hall.

Maxim laughed and said "Please contact my school. We have the best teachers there."

"We know that and we do keep asking them. But, we want to hear from you, what would you do to connect with your True-self?" asked a man sitting in the front row.

Maxim said "Hmm, what would I do? I will simply ask my True-self to make Itself known to me!"

There was a disappointed silence in the audience. Maxim laughed and said "You don't seem happy with my answer. You want something to 'do', right? Alright, let me see what can help you. I take it for granted that all of you do have an intense desire to experience your True-self, if you don't, then your True-self may keep playing hide and seek with you!"

After a short pause Maxim began "Have you practiced the method of bringing a vibrational coherence between your mind and body by meditating with your attention on your lower belly (Swadhisthan chakra) or by placing your hands on your heart? It is very effective if you combine it with slow breathing."

Maxim continued "Another good practice is to look at a picture or a candle flame or at anything that is at your eye level. After focusing your eyes at the object for few minutes, imagine you are looking back at yourself standing where the object is. Do not move your eyes or head. Later you can close your eyes, if you wish. This is a very powerful practice to become aware of your True-self."

Maxim looked around his audience and asked "Had enough?"

"No" was the reply.

He continued "We were just discussing the essential nature of our Creator. It is love, all encompassing, all including love. So, the essential nature of our True-self, which is an extension of the Creator, is also love. So, another way to connect with your True-self is by consciously feeling this mysterious creative force called love. I am sure you have heard of Sufi mystics who write poems in praise of their beloved, the Creator. Same is true for people following Bhakti Yoga. They get totally immersed in this divine stream of love. Do try it sometime. It can take you beyond this 3D reality in seconds and in the loving arms of your True-self!"

Maxim turned to look at Alaska and asked "Princess, could you help them with this process?"

Without any hesitation Alaska picked up the spare mike and said "There are many ways to connect with this divine omnipresent stream of love. The easiest way, I can think of, is, to look at yourself in a mirror and say to yourself 'I…love….you', ''I… love….you'. Keep repeating it with a gentle smile on your face and if you wish, you can keep your hand on your heart. Do remember to smile. It has a magical effect on your physical senses. It changes the very chemistry of your body. If you practice it daily for five minutes, you will discover a new dimension, the dimension of cosmic love."

As Alaska stopped speaking, Maxim said "Thank you Princess." Then he turned towards the audience and said "You must have experienced the 'flow' state, a state when you feel your best and do your best, when you transcended your limitations. Hack the 'flow' state. You must experiment to find the things that can trigger your individual 'flow' state. Usually it is something new, a bit risky, a little challenging, awe inspiring, something so beautiful that it totally arrests your attention. You forget the world! Why? Yes, you have guessed it you are one with your True-self for that moment." There was silence in the hall.

Maxim continued "Your True-self is real, not a concept, my entrepreneurs! Know it, believe it and remember it!"

After a short pause, Maxim asked "Do you have any questions that you would like to be answered before we wrap up the evening?"

"Wrap up? No, you cannot! We have hundreds of queries!" said a lady.

Maxim said "Do you have a specific question that I can clarify? Tomorrow we have another open seminar. Come and join us."

Someone quickly asked "Please tell us why we are able to manifest certain things but unable to manifest other things."

"It is mainly due to your belief, your limiting belief. You believe you are good enough for this but not for that. You believe this is possible but that is not possible. Actually your beliefs are self-prophecies. Never underestimate the vetoing power of your beliefs. What you believe becomes your reality! Your limiting beliefs can sabotage your best laid plans without you being aware of it" said Maxim.

After a moment he continued "I suggest, quit using phrases such as, we cannot, we will try, and we need. They don't behoove you, my magicians! The vibration of the words and phrases, depending upon the meaning you assign, affect your nervous system and your biology. Be diligent and choose wisely. Remember, you can make your life a work of art, if you choose to do so!"

After a short pause he continued "Another reason for not being able to manifest, is resistance to change. You do not change, you keep doing the same thing but you expect a different result. That is a recipe for disappointment, don't you think so? First, you need to change the image you have of yourself in your own mind, then, change your beliefs and so on. Always remember you are the master creator of all you perceive. Ignite a flame of love for everything you desire to create. You will have more fun. You will make your life magical if you can make yourself believe that you are a true magician, which, of course, you are!"

Maxim thought for a moment and then, asked "Do I need to remind you to watch out for doubts! Never let doubts creep in. And patience, my friends, patience! Won't you wait, as long as it takes, for your beloved to come into your life? Similarly won't you wait patiently for your dream to manifest in your life? Romance your desires as, you would, your beloved, my magicians!"

Maxim looked at his audience with a gentle smile and said "Dream, my magicians, dream, without doubting the outcome! Appreciate the beauty of your dream. Enjoy the journey. Let go! The outcome will be greater than your dream!"

When maxim stopped speaking, as usual, there was silence in the hall. Maxim waved to the audience and started walking off the stage with Alaska. The entrepreneur group came alive and gave him a standing ovation, but before Maxim and Alaska could reach the door of the hall, they were completely surrounded by the audience, and questions were pouring from all sides. Maxim laughed and said "Hold on friends, one at a time please!" Then the suggestion came from the entrepreneurs "Let us sit somewhere and have coffee together."

Maxim replied with his usual calm and gentle smile "I don't think that is a good idea. Go and be alone with yourself. Go through everything you heard this evening, feel it in your body before you forget it. If you need more clarity, contact my school and ask the teachers there. They are the best teachers available and each one of them has specialized in one aspect of spirituality. Contact them."

"No! It is not the same. We want you to clarify things for us." Was the response from the entrepreneurs.

Alaska couldn't stop giggling when she heard them. Maxim looked at Alaska with a question in his Indigo eyes. Alaska said "I totally agree with them. The teachings, the universal laws are the same but when you explain it is different. Why is it different? – I think, because, you hear what is not said, you see what is not seen and you know the unknown. Magic happens when you speak Maxim."

There was a lot of clapping with 'wow' and 'well said' from the entrepreneurs.

Maxim looked at Alaska silently for a few seconds and then murmured "I appreciate your appreciation, Princess." Then he turned towards the crowd and said "It is kind of you to invite me for coffee but you will have to excuse me this evening. I have some business work that I must attend to tonight with people in different time zones. They would be waiting for me, so I must go now. Keep your questions ready for tomorrow evening seminar. If the organizers have some objection, tell them you are my guests. I am sure they will let you attend with others."

Saying this he caught Alaska's hand and started moving towards the exit.

"Alaska, at least, you have coffee with us!" was the chorus from the entrepreneurs.

Before Alaska could open her mouth, Maxim said "I have a pile of work for her to catch up before she sleeps. I know I must appear like a villain or at best, a hard task master, but in this physical world of linear time, one has to honor time. Good night my magicians. See you tomorrow evening."

Maxim looked at the crowd with a gentle smile and walked out of the door along with Alaska.

When they reached their rooms Alaska asked "Can I meditate with you tonight Maxim?"

Maxim looked at her for a moment, and then replied "No."

Alaska looked crestfallen and asked "Why?"

Maxim replied "I have Enterprise work to do first."

"How long will it take?" asked Alaska.

"At least half hour." replied Maxim.

Alaska brightened up and said "Ok, I will come after half an hour."

"No, you will not." said Maxim.

"Why? I like to meditate with you. It is more powerful." said Alaska.

"We will meditate together in the morning." Maxim replied gently.

"Why? Why not tonight? You could have, as well, left me with the entrepreneurs to have coffee." Alaska said feeling disappointed.

Maxim asked "Did you want to?"

She mumbled "No, not without you."

Maxim smiled and said "Your physical presence distracts me. Don't you know that, Princess? I need to do some urgent Enterprise work before I sleep. And…. besides, I want to give you time, time to decide and choose who or what gives you joy. I don't want to sweep you off your feet because the outcome is never satisfactory for all concerned. I have experienced it. You are the sovereign. Take your time. Choose well."

Maxim took the room key from her hand, opened the door, went in to close the balcony door, and walked out of the room, clicking the door shut after him.

Alaska stood silently in the middle of her room with tears rolling down her cheeks. She silently said "I know what gives me joy, but I will do as you say Maxim. I will meditate till I forget you, till I forget myself and I am one with my True-self who loves me for who I am, just as I am without limitation."

Alaska meditated long and deep, after that she had a sound sleep.

****

Alaska was fast asleep when the phone rang. She jumped up and said "Hello?"

"Wake up Princess. The mighty Sun is waiting for you to come and watch it rise! Welcome the new day!" said Maxim.

"Oh, I overslept. Sorry. I will be out in five minutes." said Alaska.

She quickly washed and changed into her old Taekwondo dress and opened the door to find Maxim waiting for her outside her door. He said "Let us run to the aft of the ship. Sun would be coming out any moment."

They ran silently, hand in hand, and were soon out on the stern side deck of the ship. They stood, without saying a word and watched in awe the life-giving Sun rise out of the Atlantic. They bowed to the Sun and then, sat down on the deck and meditated together.

When they got up Alaska realized the ship had already docked at the island they were visiting today. They walked to the front of the ship. The small island looked beautiful. It was lush green with vegetation and the beach was white with blue water. They didn't see much movement on the ship. May be, most of the passengers were still asleep.

Maxim asked Alaska "Would you like to swim in one of the pools? No one would be around. Soon everyone would be heading for the island and we can have the pool to ourselves. What do you say, Princess?"

Alaska said "OK" in an absent-minded way.

Maxim looked at Alaska and asked "Why so silent Princess?"

Alaska slowly replied "I don't know. Is the island calling us?"

Maxim keenly looked at her and asked "What do you hear?"

"I don't exactly hear something, but I feel sad, Maxim. It reminds me of a woman screaming 'Jacque'. Why is she screaming Maxim?"

Maxim put his arm around her shoulder and pulled her toward himself and said "May be, because she was going to lose someone she loved. Anyway, we will not go to the island. We will stay back on the ship. OK?"

Alaska turned to look at Maxim and said "But don't you feel the island is calling you?"

Maxim replied "I feel a suppressed pain here. We don't know what happened here in the past century. May be the pirates came and looted or ravaged the island. If you feel up to it, we can disembark and find out how to free the soul of the island from all the pain and how to bring love and joy here. What do you want to do?"

"Let us go. You will bring joy and love to the island. Won't you Maxim?" asked Alaska.

"Yes, we will. Come let us have some breakfast first, then do some research about the island. When most of the passengers have gone to the island, we will try out the swimming pool, and later we will explore the island." said Maxim.

Alaska cheerfully said "Ok."

After they had their breakfast, they checked all information available about the island. It appeared that the shipping company owned the island.

When the ship appeared to be relatively silent and deserted, Maxim and Alaska headed for the bigger pool for a swim. They were surprised to see several people still there.

Alaska laughed and said "You cannot have the whole pool to yourself Maxim! Learn to share, my friend!" She teased him and splashed him with water from the pool.

Maxim said "Let me catch you!"

After swimming a few lengths, Alaska stopped and stood on the side. She realized everyone was watching them. She wished they could have had the swimming pool to themselves. Maxim came and stood beside her. He grinned reading her thoughts and said "Learn to share, my friend!"

Alaska retorted "It is your fault. You attract everyone like a magnet. They can't help but stare at you!"

Maxim laughed and said "Alright. I will go and sit on that chair. Let us see what happens then, Princess!" saying this he walked out from the pool, draped a big towel around his shoulders and sat down on one of the loungers.

Alaska didn't like it one bit. Without Maxim it was not fun. Anyway she thought she will swim for a minute or two and then get out of the pool. When she stopped, a man came to her and introduced himself. He said "I am Jonathan. I have been watching you. You are an excellent swimmer. Let us swim together. I will race you." Alaska looked around and found several people looking at her with great interest.

Alaska saw Maxim grinning from ear to ear. His wet hair was plastered on his head. He looked like a mischievous boy having great fun at her expense. Without a thought she ran out of the pool to him and tousled his wet hair. As he made to grab her, she quickly backed away and collided with a boy who came running from somewhere behind her. Alaska and the boy both slipped and fell in the pool with a big splash. Maxim jumped up and asked them "Are you ok?" When they replied "Yes", Maxim started laughing and others joined in the laughter.

Alaska realized that Jonathan was anxiously asking her "Can I help you? You must be hurt!"

Maxim could hardly stop laughing but he went into the pool, caught Alaska's hand and brought her out. Alaska was frowning at Maxim who was still grinning. He said "You did learn to share the pool, my friend! Go and change before you set the deck and the pool on fire."

Alaska frowned at Maxim and finally burst out laughing. They went to change oblivious to the admiring glances of the people around the pool.

CHAPTER 9

Maxim and Alaska walked down the gangplank of the ship on to the beautiful island. It was a bright sunny day. The island was crowded with tourists from the ship. People were sitting on the white beach under colorful umbrellas, eating, drinking and making merry. Some were swimming in the blue water of the Caribbean. Alaska turned back to look at their ship. It appeared huge and very impressive. They walked further along on the island. There were many stalls and shops selling local handicrafts. They could hear music blaring somewhere on the island. There were several dining areas serving all kinds of food and drinks. It looked festive but Alaska remembered feeling sad when she had first seen the island from the ship in the morning.

They walked on the beautiful beach, dipped their feet in the water but decided against swimming. They explored the shops selling intricately designed jewelry made of beads and shells.

Alaska asked "Maxim, could I buy some jewelry for my friends? They are beautiful. Girls would love them."

Maxim replied with a smile "Sure. Go ahead."

Alaska went from shop to shop checking bracelets, ear rings and necklaces. The shops were too crowded with tourists. Maxim stood at some distance from the shops, away from the maddening crowd of girls, but from where he could keep an eye on Alaska busy choosing trinkets. The Sun was too strong, so he found a tree and stood under its shade. He kept looking at Alaska with a smile and an indulgent look, when he realized that someone was talking to him. He found an old woman dressed like a gypsy telling him "Man, you want that woman. Take this bracelet and put it on her wrist tonight when the Moon is high in the sky and make her your own woman."

Maxim replied "No, I don't want it."

The woman said "She is beautiful. Many men want her but I see three men want her as you want her. One of them will take her away from you"

Maxim said "Don't waste your time. I will not buy anything."

"Why? You are not man enough to make her your own woman tonight when the Moon is high in the sky?" she said with a wicked gleam in her jet black eyes.

Maxim didn't want to hear her nonsense. He muttered under his breath "I am man enough to wait for my woman to come to me of her own free will."

He was surprised to see the old woman laugh like a witch and ask "So sure master?" So, the witch had obviously heard him. He looked at Alaska who was enjoying choosing the trinkets for her friends. Her face was glowing with her inner light, but she was not aware of it. She didn't know that it was her presence that was attracting dozens of people to that shop. Maxim wanted to go and stand near her to keep her safe.

The woman, who was still standing there, laughed loudly and said "Master those people will not harm her but I see three men who want to take her away from you. One man has dark hair, the other has light hair and the third is not from our world, and master, you know them."

Saying this, the woman went away but was back soon with a long string of multi colored crystals and sea shells. She said to Maxim "Take this master and give it to her tonight when the Moon is high in the sky. I not lie to you. I know you are a master. You see beyond the veils of death. You talk to God. You know what everyman thinks. Take it."

Maxim wondered how much she could actually see and how much was sales talk. He looked at Alaska, who was still busy with the jewelry.

He said "Can you tell me the names of the three men you were talking about?"

The woman replied "Give me a little time master to get the pictures of the men in my head. Then you can see what I see."

Maxim once again looked at Alaska and then said to the woman "OK. Go ahead and get the pictures in your head, now!"

His full attention was on the woman and he was surprised to clearly see the pictures of Mark, the dark one, Brian, the fair one and of Jacque. For a moment there was silence. The woman asked "Master, can you see?"

Maxim replied "Yes. So, you can actually see the past and the future, then why do you talk such rubbish – make her your woman when the Moon is high etc. etc.?"

The woman replied "What can I do? Tourists want a story- true or false, only then they feel happy and buy our beads, and I get money to eat."

Maxim asked her "Tell me where you learned to see the unseen future?"

The woman replied "My grandmother taught me. She was a witch. But my island is poor. We are poor."

Maxim said "I have a spiritual school in America. Would you like to come to America and teach other people how to see the unseen as your grandmother taught you?"

Just then Alaska came running to Maxim and said "Sorry, I took so long. They have got such beautiful things. Maxim, could you please lend me 50 dollars? I left my wallet on the ship."

Alaska saw the long string that the woman was still holding in her hands. She asked Maxim "Did you buy something from her? That is a very unusual string. It is beautiful."

The woman quickly hid the string in her bag. Alaska was surprised. She looked at Maxim. He shrugged his shoulders and gave her the cash with a smile.

The moment Alaska left, the woman said "Master hide it in your pocket. Give it to her only when the Moon is high in the sky. Moon controls our mind. Believe me!"

Maxim took the string with a smile and put it in his pocket saying "OK, you win."

He said to the old woman "Give me your name and address. I will send a man who will bring you to my school in America."

The woman said wistfully "Master, I have no money. I have no papers. How can I come to America?"

Alaska finally came back happy with the things she had bought.

Maxim replied to the woman "You give me your name and address, rest I will do."

The woman had tears in her eyes. She asked "Really master? Really you will send someone to take me to America? I have no money master!"

Alaska gently said "Don't you know master is a magician? Whatever he says happens. So, quickly give your name and address to him."

The woman said "I will get a boy to write my address and then I will come. Wait for me, my queen!"

Alaska was surprised to hear herself addressed as queen. She asked Maxim when the woman had left "Did you buy something from her? I saw you chatting with her."

Maxim replied vaguely "nothing much."

The woman soon came back and gave him a piece of paper. Maxim checked the paper and asked "You are Maria?"

She nodded her head and said "Yes master."

Maxim took out a visiting card and signed it at the back and gave it to the woman saying "Keep this card. When my man comes, give him this card and he will bring you to America." He remembered he had not paid Maria for the string. He gave her $100 because she had not told him the price of the string. She put the money and the card inside her blouse and said "Tonight master! Don't forget!"

Before leaving Maria looked at Alaska from head to toe. She nodded her head in approval and said to no one in particular "Good wife for my master." and went away laughing loudly.

Alaska asked "Something wrong with her?"

Maxim grinned and said "Well, yes. She is a witch. She can see the unseen."

"What? Can she really?" exclaimed Alaska.

"Yes, that is why I am getting her to teach at my school. Are you thirsty? It is very warm here." asked Maxim.

Alaska said "Yes, please. Let us find somewhere to sit and drink something cool."

They found a counter serving fresh fruit juices and coconut water. They picked up 2 coconuts and sat near a pedestal fan to sip it.

Maxim casually asked "How is Mark?"

Alaska replied "Well, he must be ok. Why do you ask?"

Maxim replied "No reason. Do you have any friend called Brian?"

Alaska thought for a moment and said "No, I don't unless you count Brian whom I met in your office in Boston. He is a friend of yours, isn't he? He is nice. I like him. Actually he calls me whenever he is in Boston."

Maxim smiled and said "Yes, he is a friend of mine."

When they finished their coconut water, they explored the island for some time. They came to a big circular hall with many little shops selling local handicraft and dresses inside it. The place looked very crowded, so Alaska said to Maxim "You stay here. I will have a quick look inside and come back."

Maxim asked "You want to go in?"

Alaska asked "Can I?"

Maxim smiled and said "Sure! Let us brave the crowd together, shall we?"

They walked in together. Alaska looked around the shops full of local handicrafts. She saw a counter where beautiful long ear rings made of colored crystals were displayed. She managed to squeeze in through the crowd to the counter. Alaska chose a pair made of turquoise stones set in white metal. She put it on and showed it to Maxim. Maxim looked at her and said "Beautiful. Take it."

But when Alaska asked the girl at the counter to give it, she said "This is sold. But I can find another pair like this for you, if you really want it. The price of this new pair is $200."

Alaska objected "200? Why? You have written $20 for each pair!"

Just then Alaska felt a tug on her arm. She saw a little boy pulling her. Maxim saw him and asked "Yes? What do you want?"

The boy pointed towards the exit of the hall and said in a whisper "Mother calls you."

Maxim said to Alaska "Let us go and see what this boy is talking about."

As they moved from the counter, the girl called them back. The boy again pulled at her arm and pointed towards the exit.

Maxim said "Let us go Princess and see what it is all about."

They followed the boy. Just outside the hall, they met a woman, presumably the boy's mother. She took out several pairs of long dangling ear rings made of stones from her bag. She said "I make the ear rings. She sells it inside for $20. She gives me $3 for each pair."

Alaska asked "Why don't you sell it yourself inside the hall?"

The woman replied "I have no money. They ask big money for shop."

Maxim looked at Alaska. Alaska nodded her head.

Maxim said to the woman "Write your name, address on a paper and give it to me. Next month I will send a man here. He will meet you and buy a shop inside the hall for you so that you can sell your jewelry inside and earn more money. OK?"

The woman replied "I don't have money to rent a shop."

Maxim replied "You will not have to rent it. The shop is a gift to you from this Princess."

The woman, silently, kept looking at them.

Alaska gently said "We need your name and address."

Maxim took out another visiting card, signed it and gave it to the woman saying "Next month my man will come here. You give this card to him and he will buy a shop and give it to you. This shop is a gift from us. You don't need to pay for it."

The woman wiped her eyes and said "I thought God had forgotten us. But God has come today. Master you have come. Master, send my son to school. Here only one school. They tell me no place for my son."

Maxim replied "OK, but first give me your name and address. Write your son's name too on the paper."

The woman said something to her son who ran away to get the address, thought Alaska. The woman took out two pairs of long dangling ear rings, one of green stones and the other of black shiny stones and said to Maxim "Master take this for your Princess. Look beautiful!"

Maxim looked at Alaska and asked her "Princess?"

"They are beautiful, but, I wonder when I can wear them, may be, I can give these to my friends."

Maxim said "No, you keep these and wear them. You can buy more for your friends, if you wish."

The boy came back running and gave a piece of paper to Maxim.

Maxim checked the paper. He took out a $100 bill and gave it to the woman.

He said "Keep the card that I gave you safe. Without my card, my man cannot buy a shop for you or send your son to school."

The woman returned the $100 bill saying "Master $20 for both the ear rings."

Maxim smiled and said "Keep the money. Have a good dinner with your family."

The woman took the money and said "Master come again. We need a God who can hear us."

Maxim gently said "Next month my man will come here. He will sort out your problems."

She replied "Thank you master. But you come. You are the unknown God, my mother used to say, will come one day and our island will be happy again."

Maxim looked at Alaska with a question in his Indigo eyes. Alaska looked at the woman gazing at Maxim with complete trust.

Involuntarily Alaska heard herself say to the woman "Celebrate Josephine! All pain has been washed away. Rejoice! Your God has awakened!"

The woman was stunned to hear it and looked at Alaska with wide opened eyes, as if she couldn't believe what she had heard.

Maxim looked at Alaska with a gentle smile. He was not surprised at her prophecy. He knew Alaska's powers although she herself was not aware of it.

The woman finally managed to ask Alaska "How did you know my birth name is Josephine? I know, I know, I know…..God has answered our prayer, God has come!"

Alaska was trying hard to think what made her say Josephine, but before she could come to a conclusion, they were joined by five people from the successful entrepreneur group. They said "We have been looking for your two since morning. Thank God, we, at last found you."

Maxim replied "We came to the island quite late."

One of the two girls from the group asked Alaska "Have you bought those ear rings from this woman?" She had seen the ear rings Alaska was still holding in her hands.

Alaska showed her ear rings and said "Josephine makes these jewelry. They are beautiful and cost only $10 a pair."

Josephine opened her bag and showed them her jewelry. Both the girls from the group got busy choosing and buying things from her.

The remaining three men from the group introduced themselves to Maxim and asked him "How do we address you- Gladiator or Mr. De Winter?"

Maxim replied with a smile "Mmm… well, my name is Maxim De Winter, so, that seems appropriate."

By now the two girls had finished buying the jewelry and joined the group. Josephine closed her bag and said to Maxim "Master, come back soon. The island awaits you!" and left them.

Five pairs of eyes were looking at Maxim curiously.

Maxim asked them "You said you were looking for us since morning. Any special reason?"

The girl called Julie Anne replied "We explored the island as much as we could in a day. Although it looks festive with music etc., the local people don't seem happy. They seem kind of oppressed. We wondered, can't we do something for them? May be, we could start some business here, set up some industry. What do you think Mr. De Winter?"

Maxim replied "As far as I know, this island is owned by the shipping company. Why do the natives seem oppressed? You will need to research all the legal implications. What nationality the natives have? Buying an island of this size will not be a problem for De Winter Enterprises."

All five answered in unison "Mr. De Winter we will do it. We will do all the research for you. If you are with us, we will make a success of it."

Maxim replied "Each one of us will do individual research and come up with our own ideas to help the natives. Will two months be enough for your detailed research?"

"Yes." was the enthusiastic answer.

Maxim said "Alright. Contact me when you are ready." He gave them his visiting card and added "Do write 'cruise island project' prominently on your reports"

All five of them were looking excited about the island project. They couldn't believe that Maxim had agreed to work with them and help them financially or even buy the island. The entrepreneurs didn't know that Maxim had already decided to help the natives before they came up with the island project idea.

Maxim said to Alaska "Come on Princess, time for work. Let us go back to the ship now."

Alaska was surprised and the other five were disappointed to hear it.

The entrepreneurs said "There is enough time. Can't we have a drink before we go back to the ship? It sails at 5PM, isn't it?"

Maxim replied "Yes, that is true but I have some work to complete before the evening seminar. See you at 7!" Saying this, Maxim, along with Alaska, walked back to the ship.

When they boarded the ship Alaska asked "Maxim, why don't you want to sit and chat with the entrepreneurs? They ask you again and again but you keep giving them some excuse or the other. Maxim, I wonder if you know how good it feels just to be in your presence! Why do you deny them?"

They stopped walking. Maxim turned towards Alaska and looked at her deeply with a gentle, indulgent expression in his Indigo eyes. Alaska looked at him with eyes wide open. She didn't know how long they stood there looking at each other.

She came to the present with a jerk when Maxim softly said "Breathe Princess!" and tucked a strand of her hair behind her ear. He caught her hand and started walking. With a teasing smile he said "Don't you know why, Princess? Tomorrow at this time, physically, we would be thousands of miles apart!"

Alaska looked at him and held on to his hand with all her might.

They went up to the main restaurant. It was nearly empty as most of the passengers were still on the island. Maxim ordered Alaska's favorite burger with potato wedges and cold coffee. They ate it leisurely all the while discussing last evening's seminar. When they finished Alaska took out everything she had bought at the island for her friends.

Maxim asked her "Your friends? What about me? Don't I count?"

Alaska said "I thought you may not wear it. Will you?"

"You will have to give it first." murmured Maxim.

Alaska took out a bracelet made of silky blue thread with Indigo blue stones which she had deliberately not taken out of the bag. She put it on, on Maxim's right wrist.

Maxim said "I am glad you thought of me. Very fond of Indigo color, aren't you?"

Alaska smiled and shyly nodded her head in agreement.

Maxim thought of the long string that Maria had sold to him. He wanted to give it to Alaska now, but he could almost hear Maria saying "give it tonight when the moon is high in the sky." Maria you are a witch. You have won. Ok, I will give it to Princess when the Moon is high in the sky.

Alaska took out the long dangling ear rings she had bought from Josephine. Maxim picked up the ear ring with green stones and said "Wear it tonight."

Alaska said "Tonight? Won't I look over dressed for the seminar? I rarely wear jewelry. I am not used to it."

Maxim said "Then get used to it. I have got piles of jewelry lying in bank lockers, thanks to my two grand-mothers, who, obviously, were very fond of jewelry."

Alaska asked curiously "Really? I would love to meet them."

"Well, they are not alive, not in the physical world anyway. My ancestors didn't believe in long lives." replied Maxim.

Maxim got up saying "We should head for our rooms. It is time to shower and get dressed for the seminar, Princess."

While walking back to their rooms, Alaska thought 'Maxim could have piles of jewelry but that doesn't mean I can wear them. Isn't it like presuming, just because he has got piles of money, I can spend it. Or, can I?'

Alaska was startled to hear "Yes, you can."

Alaska turned to look at Maxim and found him grinning from ear to ear.

She grumbled "Hey, Maxim, you read all my thoughts. It is not fair!"

Maxim answered "It is more than fair. You got the answer to a question that you didn't bother to ask, and, as I have said many times, you are welcome to read my thoughts, if you so wished."

By now they had reached their rooms. Maxim opened the door for Alaska and said "Do telephone your mother first and then get ready. See you Princess."

Alaska was ready by 6.45. She opened her door to find Maxim waiting for her. As always, he looked handsome in his impeccable suit and blue shirt. His magnetism was palpable. She smiled and said "Hey Maxim you look so attractive. No wonder everyone stares at you!?

Maxim bowed to her and said "Thank you gracious lady. Let me look at you. You, as usual, are breath-taking, but somehow, different today."

Alaska shook her head and showed her dangling ear rings she was wearing.

Maxim said "Ah, the ear rings! And your hair. What have you done?"

Alaska replied "Nothing much, just tied it up so that the ear rings can show."

Maxim softly said "I didn't know you had such a beautiful neck." He kept looking at her. Alaska knew her face was turning pink under his intense admiring gaze. She hastily said "Let us go. We will be late."

Maxim laughed and started walking towards the auditorium. He said "Princess, you look so dainty and fragile, I worry you may melt away if I touched you."

Alaska mumbled while walking as fast as she could to keep up with Maxim "No, I won't."

Maxim laughed and said "I will have to check sometime."

When they reached the auditorium, Alaska was astounded to see it over-flowing with hundreds or was it thousands, of people sitting and standing around the hall.

Alaska stopped for a second and clutched at Maxim's hand murmuring "Oh Maxim!"

Maxim softly said "Princess, it is you! Your spiritual magnetism will always attract people in hoards. Let us give them our best. Let us awaken, each one of them, to their own inherent powers, to realize that they are gods, that, they have the magical power to create whatever they desire. We have to shake them out of their comfort zone and break free from the limiting beliefs."

On way to the stage, Maxim picked up a bottle of lemonade for Alaska. When they reached the stage, they were met with a rousing welcome. The clapping went on for a minute or two. Maxim waved his hand with his usual nonchalant smile while the assistant fixed the little mike. Alaska sat on a chair on the stage with closed eyes sensing the vibration of the audience.

When the clapping stopped, Maxim stood silently for a few seconds sensing the vibration of his audience.

Maxim began "Tell me my friends, what, you would like me to say, that will set you afire with an unbridled desire to know yourself?"

A lady, in her forties, got up and said "You say we are powerful beyond measure. Well, where is the power? Where is the magic? I couldn't care less about who I am. I am interested in the power you say we have, power to create our own reality, our dreams."

Maxim said "Ah, the power. So, it is the power that sets you afire. Well, you are right- Know thy power, it will set you free, absolutely free from all imagined limitations. Yes, all limitations are imagined. Well, there is a little problem here. You want to jump straight to power without, first, experiencing who or what you are. Power comes naturally to you, once you know who or what you are. But you just said you couldn't care less to learn who or what you are! Well, in that case, you will have to take my word for it, that, you are a non-physical being, and like a true magician, you are creating, manifesting, and generating the things you desire just by desiring it, literally out of thin air!"

Maxim paused and looked at the lady who had asked the question. As the lady remained silent he continued "From your statement, I take it, you have not been able to manifest your desires, your dreams. Am I right?"

The lady replied "yes."

Maxim said "It is your flawed beliefs my friend. It makes you doubt your own magical powers of creation. It doesn't let you believe that it is you, only you, who is creating your perceived reality. Change your belief, change your life! You need to shift your identity from being a helpless human, who is always wistfully wishing for the fulfilment of a dream, to a powerful creator. Take back your power that you handed over to others or to a supposedly punishing god who is beyond your reach."

Maxim paused and waited for a comment from the lady, but there was none. So, he continued "Know that your boss, your spouse, your family, your society, your country, this world is not your banker, your True-self is! Whether you are looking for abundance or enlightenment, don't expect it to come from outside of you. This reality, that you perceive, has been created by you. Believe it!"

After a short pause Maxim continued "You may face some resistance from your sub-conscious mind when you change your identity, your self-image, because it thinks a change may not be safe for you, but if you are passionate about your dream, you will break the barrier of this resistance and accomplish the change necessary for the manifestation of your desire and/or the new you that is powerful beyond comprehension of your mind."

Maxim continued "I trust you know the formula –
DREAM
FOLLOW YOUR DREAM
LIVE THE LIFE OF YOUR DREAMS

Let go of all limiting beliefs, all doubts. The Universe will deliver your dream in its perfect time. Feel the joy of your dream already in your life, before you see it in your perceived reality."

As Maxim stopped, a question came "What do you mean by 'dream'?"

Maxim replied with his gentle smile "A dream is a desire that you love, that you are passionate about, that makes you come alive."

"You always say 'you are the ultimate magician'. Why?" was the next question.

Maxim said "Ah, my friend, you have spoken like the magician who has forgotten that he has magic at his fingertips!"

He smiled and looked at his audience and said "Well, I call you the ultimate magician because you are one! You are the ultimate creators! You are gods! You have the ultimate power to choose and decide what you want to create! You came with powers to create anything you desired, literally out of thin air! The problem is you were never told about it either at home or at your school, so, today you cannot bring yourself to believe it, although you are endowed with this un-imaginable creative power by the Creator with unconditional love for you."

Alaska admired Maxim's patience. She wondered how he remained calm while explaining the same basic spiritual truth again and again and again. He never became annoyed or irritated. He remained his gentle, smiling self, no matter what the question was!

Maxim gave his audience time to digest the information that he had just given to them. Then he asked "Would you like me to elaborate a little on the topic of the magician?"

"Yes" was the immediate response from the audience.

He continued "Alright. Let us begin with 'magic'. What is magic? Magic is a thing or a process that your logical mind is unable to grasp, to understand, or to explain how or why, it happens."

"Now, then, who is a magician? A magician is a person who creates something out of nothing, out of thin air, so to speak, or, who does something extra-ordinary, the process of which is not understood by the masses."

"Please do not confuse the ultimate magicians with people who, for the purpose of fun and/or entertainment, produce a rabbit seemingly out of thin air by tricks or sleight of hand. Ultimate magicians can actually produce a live rabbit literally out of thin air because they have the divine creative power to do so and they know it!"

"Would you like to know why I specially use the word 'ultimate'? I use the word 'ultimate' because, the Creator did not create anyone superior to you my magicians! You are the last word, you are the final word in creation! You are the ultimate magicians, the ultimate creators- know it, acknowledge it, and believe it."

Maxim stopped and looked around. Alaska was surprised to hear the next question. It came from a lady in a wheel-chair. She asked "Can I ask you a question, young man?"

Maxim gave her a beautiful, disarming smile and said "Sure, beautiful lady."

"Tell me, how did you become the way you are- -handsome, charismatic, almost irresistible, and I am told, you are a billionaire to boot? How did you achieve this deadly combination of knowledge, wealth and magnetic presence? Did you dream, then, follow your dream, as you preach?"

There was silence in the hall. Everyone was curious to hear the answer.

Maxim laughed and replied "No, because that never was my dream! And by the way, thank you for your compliments."

The old lady laughed and said "This is not an idle curiosity. My grand-son admires you and hopes to become someone like you. Could you help him?" She pointed towards a young man sitting by her side, who was looking extremely uncomfortable with his eyes fixed on his boots.

Maxim looked at the grand-son and said "No need to feel so uncomfortable. Look up my friend so I can see you."

The young man hesitated at first with his eyes down cast, but soon mustered enough courage to look up. Alaska saw Maxim give him one of his intense unwavering look for almost a minute. She knew he must be reading the man like an open book and clearing away his blocks.

After a few seconds, Maxim smiled and said "You are the ultimate magician, my friend, believe it, and feel it! Now, visualize your dream with all the passion in your heart. Demand it with unshakeable faith. Your dream will manifest in its own perfect time. You must meditate every day, to consciously connect and be one with your True-self, your inner magician, and you will enjoy the life of your dreams. Never doubt!"

The moment Maxim stopped speaking, the young man jumped up grinning from ear to ear saying "Thank you Gladiator, thank you Gladiator, thank you, thank you, thank you!"

His grand-mother looked at him askance. The young man said "I told you grand-ma, Gladiator is a magician. He has done magic, can't you feel it?"

Maxim laughed and said "So are you! Remember to meditate every day. Check with my spiritual school. They will teach the meditations that will help you become aware of and remain aware of your True-self 24/7."

The old lady asked "What did you do Gladiator? Are you really a magician?"

Maxim replied with his usual smile "Yes, I am and so are you!"

The woman asked vehemently "Then why am I wheel-chair bound? Why can't I get up and walk?"

Maxim replied "You can, if you want to."

The woman said indignantly "What? What do you mean? You think I don't want to walk?"

Maxim said "You want to, but you believe you cannot and so, you do not."

The woman was shocked to hear it and said "What?"

Her grand-son quickly intervened and said "Please, please Gladiator, please do something and make her walk. Please!"

Maxim laughed and said "You know the formula – dream, then follow your dream and then, live the life of your dreams! Simple! My beautiful lady, I take it, your dream is to walk again. You have an intense desire to walk, run, and jump. You are passionate about it. Just the thought of walking makes you come alive! If that is the case, if that is true, then, first meditate for a few minutes to bring coherence between the vibrations of your mind and body. When your analytical mind becomes calm, visualize and feel as if you are walking confidently around your home, in stores, on side-walks, for as long as you can, irrespective of your current physical situation. Feel the joy and freedom of walking on your own, before, I repeat, before, you actually do it in this physical reality! Don't let any doubt creep in. Rest assured, if you practice it daily and you can believe that you are the creator of your reality, soon you will be walking briskly with your grand-son. Your belief, your thoughts, your feelings create your so called, reality."

Maxim paused and looked at Alaska who had been listening to him with full attention. He smiled at her and continued "Do you know why people get sick? Germs and viruses don't make them sick it is their thoughts and beliefs that make them sick! People suffer from cancer and numerous chronic diseases. Do you know why? They suffer from these diseases because they have stored the emotional pain of hurt, humiliation, insults, criticism, physical and emotional traumas in their bodies, which, later develop as deadly diseases. My friends, you can cure any disease by changing your thoughts and beliefs."

Maxim paused for a few moments, then, continued "Awaken my magicians to your God given powers, the powers you were born with. You are not separate from the one Creator. Stop competing with other humans for survival. Forget Darwin's theory of survival of the fittest or the strongest. You are all fit to thrive, let alone survive."

"Venture out of 3D physical world of cause and effect. It is time for you to move on to the quantum field where you, with your thoughts and beliefs, cause the effect."

"Acknowledge your powers. Love yourself, celebrate yourself my ultimate magicians! You are worth it!"

As usual, there was silence when Maxim stopped speaking. With a wave of his hand to the audience Maxim moved towards Alaska, and again, as usual, then, came the applause. Clapping went on and soon they were surrounded by hundreds of people with questions for Maxim.

Maxim raised his hands and said "Answer to all your questions are available at my website. You are welcome to visit my school and we would be more than happy to help you on your spiritual path."

Next question was "Can we meet you?"

Maxim smiled and said "If need be, yes." Saying this he started moving towards the exit. A couple came forward and said "We didn't know a spiritual seminar could be like this. It was wonderful. Now we are going to follow you and attend as many of your seminars as possible. Today we learned a lot. We will catch you in your next seminar with our questions."

Maxim laughed and said "Thank you. I am looking forward to it."

Maxim and Alaska had barely taken a step out of the exit door when they saw the five entrepreneurs standing there, waiting for them. Alaska couldn't stop laughing. Maxim looked at her and murmured "Having fun, aren't you?"

The entrepreneurs said "Please have coffee with us. Today is the last day of the seminar and the cruise. Please!"

One of them said "I know it is impossible to meet you Mr. De Winter. I have been trying to make an appointment to see you for the past 12 months, but, always, the answer is 'He is not available'."

Maxim gently said "Thanks for your invitation. I appreciate it but I have to catch up with the Enterprise work. You will have to excuse us for now but I have a better idea. Why don't you all come and join us in our morning meditation at 5?"

"Yes, we will love to join you. Where do we have to come?" was the response.

Maxim replied "Open deck on the aft of the ship. Do remember to get yoga mats from your rooms to sit on the floor." Saying this, as they made to move, two girls from the group said "No, Mr. De Winter, you are not going to leave us like this. Please have coffee with us."

Alaska felt sorry for them and said "Maxim, they have asked you so many times. Actually you have no idea how good it feels to be in your magnetic presence."

Maxim laughed and softly asked "Really?"

Alaska nodded her head and held on to his hand and said "Yes. Come for half an hour."

Hearing this everyone said "Yes, for half an hour, please!"

Five pairs of eyes were fixed on them. When Maxim didn't say anything, Alaska looked up at him and gently shook his hand.

Maxim smiled and slowly said "Your wish is my command Princess. Where do you want to have coffee?"

They went to one of the coffee shops on the top deck. It was late, so, thankfully it was not over-crowded. They joined two tables so that they all could sit together.

Maxim told Alaska "I will get something to drink for us." Saying this he went to the coffee counter. Others discussed what to have and finally followed him to the counter. Two of them remained behind with Alaska. They introduced themselves. The man said "I am Brian." And the woman said "I am Judith."

Alaska remembered Maxim's advice not to shake hands lest her high frequency make them feel uncomfortable. She gave them her dazzling smile and said "I am Alaska. Nice to meet you."

Then, Brian surprised her by asking "Are you engaged to Mr. De Winter?"

"What? No, of course not!" retorted Alaska. She turned to look at Maxim who was laughing openly with a wicked gleam in his Indigo eyes. She heard him say "Another Brian? Have mercy, my Lord! Carry on Princess, I am not listening!" with a big grin. That annoyed Alaska so much, she marched straight to Maxim and said "Stop laughing if you don't want the coffee poured over your head!"

Maxim reached over to Alaska and tucked a strand of hair behind her ear and softly said "Coffee is nearly ready. Go to the table. I am coming."

When Alaska came back to the table, Brian was nowhere to be seen. Soon rest of them returned to the table and introduced themselves. They chatted about the cruise and the entertainment provided on board the ship. Maxim hadn't come. Alaska wondered where he had disappeared to. She got up to investigate when she saw him coming back with a loaded tray. He had brought vegie pizza, a plate of French fries and two glasses of cold coffee topped up with swirls of vanilla ice-cream. Alaska forgot her annoyance when she saw the tray full of food. She said "Hey, Maxim, how did you know I was hungry?"

Maxim sat down with his coffee and said with a smile "We missed our dinner tonight, remember?"

"I think I will also have some pizza." said Vicky from the group. In the end all of them had Pizza, French fries and coffee.

The entrepreneurs discussed their passions with Maxim and told him about their businesses. After some time Maxim asked them "What about your families? You have not said a word about your partners or your friends."

When he was informed that none of them were married or had a serious relationship, he gently asked "Why? Are you too focused on your ambition, your success at work? No time for romance and love? Love is our final frontier. Stop the relentless race to imaginary finish lines! Stop this unquenchable thirst for more! Slow down and turn within! There you will find the presence of your True-self, the unknown lover, as I call it sometimes! You don't know what you are missing. If you have not experienced the joy of closing the gap between you and your beloved, then you have not experienced the Divine! Yes, love is divine."

After a short pause Maxim asked "What about you Brian? You too haven't had any time for love or you haven't found the right one who could set your pulses on fire?"

Brian slowly replied "I found the right one, but she is not free."

Maxim said with a smile "Don't be so down-cast my friend. You are an ultimate magician. You can create the life of your dreams."

Brian immediately said "But I don't want a life without my girl, my dream-girl. Can I create my dream-girl? Can I, Mr. De Winter?"

After looking keenly at Brian, Maxim replied "Yes, you can. Everything you perceive is your creation but when you choose to come in this physical world, you are limited by the physical laws such as time and space. If you have patience, persistence and above all, love for your dream-girl, then, yes, you can attract and bring her in your life Brian. I trust you know that love is within you, not out there. You are whole and complete. You don't need someone else to come in your life to make you whole. Your dream-girl is a trigger to awaken you to divine love."

The silence that ensued was surprisingly broken by Judith. She asked "Mr. De Winter everyone knows you are the most eligible bachelor, but do you have a fiancée or may be, have a special girl-friend?"

Maxim replied with a smile "No, I don't have a fiancée."

Judith persisted. She asked "Then, you are.....free?"

Maxim said "No, I am not free, as you put it, because my heart is engaged. It has been engaged for eons."

"Oh." said Judith confused. Alaska wondered what Maxim did mean?

Then Neil, another guy from the group, asked "Mr. De Winter, I always imagine the worst possible scenario whenever I am not sure of the outcome. What can I do about it?"

Maxim said "Scientists say human brain is hard-wired to always imagine the worst scenario because it wants to keep you safe. It doesn't want you to take any risk. Neil you have to make new neuro pathways in your brain and hard-wire it to imagine the best possible outcomes in every kind of situation. I think you can make a new neuro pathway in 21 days. Have an optimistic mind set, no matter what. Make it a habit to expect miracles, and your life will become miraculous!"

Maxim smiled and said "Come on Princess, let us go. It is late."

Judith quickly asked "Mr. De Winter, please tell us something, something that will help us in our life."

Maxim smiled and said "First and foremost, get clear on what you want. What is your dream? Do you wake up every morning on fire to get on with your 'dream'?"

"Second, if you are looking for joy, you must turn within, towards your True-self because that is where it is generated."

"Third, you are entrepreneurs, so, obviously you want to go beyond your genetic destiny. Am I right? So, if you want to effortlessly succeed in this 3D world in quantum leaps, you need to tap into your boundless spiritual powers."

Next question was from Mac. He said "Do we need to meditate to tap into our spiritual power?"

Maxim laughed and said "Yes, that is the easiest way to calm your over analytical mind, my friend!"

"Must we always close eyes to meditate?" asked Judith.

"No, it is not necessary to close your eyes to meditate. One of the most powerful meditations is done with eyes open. It is your choice." replied Maxim.

He got up and said "All your questions can be answered at the school. It is late. Good night my friends. See you tomorrow morning." Saying this Maxim and Alaska left.

****

When they reached their rooms Alaska looked at Maxim for a second but without saying anything, opened her door and went in. She remembered what had happened last night when she had asked to meditate with him, so she decided not to ask again.

She changed and was brushing her teeth when she heard her phone ring. She looked at it and was surprised to see it was from Maxim. She picked up the phone and said "Hello?"

Maxim asked "Where were you? I knocked at your door so many times."

Alaska asked "Where are you?"

He replied "In front of your door."

She quickly opened her door with her toothbrush in hand and tooth paste all around her mouth. Maxim laughed when he saw her. He said "I would have waited for few more minutes, anyway, go and wash." Saying this he went out to the balcony and stood looking at the Moon.

Alaska couldn't believe that Maxim had come. She washed quickly and went out to join Maxim on the balcony.

Maxim said "Look at the full moon Princess."

Alaska looked and said "WOW! Doesn't it look too big tonight Maxim?"

Maxim replied "Yes, it does. I think it is the time when Moon is nearest to Earth."

Saying this he took out the long string that Maria had given him, from his pocket. Alaska saw it and exclaimed "Hey Maxim, you bought it! Why didn't you show it to me?"

Maxim took her hand and wrapped the string several times round her wrist and tied it in a strong knot and then replied "I had to tie it when the Moon was high up in the sky showering you with its love and beauty."

Alaska admired the multi-colored crystals hanging from the string. She found a little silver box attached to the string that made a sound when she shook her hand.

Maxim was watching her. He said "I believe the box is filled with flower seeds to enhance your creativity."

"Really?" asked Alaska looking at Maxim with awe.

"Really." Maxim softly said. He once again looked at the giant Moon and said "Come Princess, let us go in."

As they walked in the room, Maxim closed the balcony door and walked out of the front door, saying "Don't take off the string tonight. I will help you take it off tomorrow."

Alaska was surprised and said "I won't. It is so beautiful. But why?"

Maxim laughed and said before closing her front door "because the witch said not to!"

Alaska kept looking at the closed door for a second, then looked at the string securely tied to her wrist. She touched it and felt immensely happy, she was not sure why. She kept seeing Maxim's laughing Indigo eyes, when she suddenly heard "Stop looking at me Princess. You know you are distracting me. Now, you meditate, then, I will finish my work quickly and meditate too."

Alaska knew nothing could ever fluster Maxim. He was always calm, cool, his smiling-self. Could she really distract him? She felt a peculiar sense of power. Could she really?

'Yes, you could and you do. No more talk, little one' was the silent answer she got.

She hugged the string to her heart and sat down to meditate.

CHAPTER 10

Alaska was on board the flight going back to Boston from Miami. She was missing Maxim awfully. She didn't know how the two days with Maxim on the cruise had flown by. She didn't remember what all they did, but it had been out of this world for her. This trip was the longest that she had stayed with Maxim and now she was missing him awfully.

Today at 4.30 AM Maxim had called her and said "Wake up sleeping beauty. Remember, we have a meditation rendezvous to keep? If you can come quickly, we can be all by ourselves on the deck and see the sky change colors before the others arrive and the mighty Sun showers us with its bounty."

Alaska was instantly awake. She had quickly washed and changed and opened the door to find Maxim waiting for her. They silently ran to the deck on the aft of the ship and stood there looking at the sky. The breeze on the deck was blowing Alaska's hair all over her face. Maxim smoothed it back and stood behind her gently supporting her. Alaska leaned back against him. She had never felt such peace in her life. Was it peace or was it a sense of being cherished beyond reason? She didn't know. She didn't care. They had stood like that for several minutes before the entrepreneurs had come. Maxim had given them some instruction for the meditation, and then they had meditated together.

After the meditation Alaska and Maxim had gone for a quick breakfast. The ship had already docked. They could see Miami's beautiful skyline from the restaurant. Soon they had disembarked from the ship and went to the airport to catch their flights. Alaska had called her parents while Maxim had dropped their bags at the airlines counter. He had bought coffee for them. They had walked to the departure gate of her flight. Maxim's flight was an hour later. Alaska had stood silently sipping her coffee. Maxim had asked "Why so silent Princess?"

When she had not said anything, he had said "Look up Princess, we shall meet again."

She had asked "When?"

And he had asked with a smile "When do you want to see me?"

She had laughed at the memory of this dialogue and had replied "Soon."

And Maxim had said very softly "Your wish is my command Princess." He hugged her and had said "Your flight is boarding. Come. Mr. Mendoza would be waiting at the airport for you. He will drive you to your dorm."

After a little pause he had continued "Do let me know how many admirers you collected on the flight." She had smiled and he had said "Smile, Princess, always smile. Let your smile change the world. Radiate so much love that no one is left unhappy on this planet." Saying this he had hugged her for a second and she had left to board her flight to Boston.

She knew Maxim was completely oblivious to the curious, interested gaze of other passengers and the airline staff, and she was surprised to realize that, now, it didn't bother her as much as it used to. And now she was travelling back to Boston and missing Maxim.

****

As soon as she reached her dorm she called her parents as Maxim had suggested her to do. She gave them all the details of the seminars on board the cruise. She talked about the island visit and the jewelry she had bought. Finally her mother asked "Tell me Aly, how Gladiator behaves with you on these seminar trips?"

Alaska thought for a second and then replied "Mom, he behaves as he always does. He is gentle, kind and considerate. He never left me alone with anyone on the ship. He ensured I had enough to eat. And I loved to meditate with him early in the morning on the deck watching the Sun rise out of Atlantic Ocean. Mom, don't worry. I don't know how to tell you, but Maxim cares! He will never hurt me or, for that matter, anybody else."

****

After the exciting cruise with Maxim, life at the college seemed very tame. Anyway, Alaska soon settled back in the college routine. But, some things had changed. Now, Maxim always told her about his whereabouts. She knew which part of the world and time zone he was in, although she never called him. He called her often enough and shared all the news about his forthcoming seminars. He made her laugh telling her funny anecdotes from his official conferences. He would always ask about her parents, her friends and her studies. She would excitedly look forward to his calls. Sometimes when she missed him too much, she would silently sit and focus on his Indigo eyes, and sure enough, he would call and say "Your wish is my command Princess. What can I do for you?"

Sometimes when he was busy he would say he will call later and he did.

Alaska was busy with her upcoming exam. Her parents wanted her to visit them on the next weekend, but she hoped Maxim would come although he had not said anything about his visit to Boston.

Alaska was on way to her next class when she sensed something on her neck. She looked over her shoulder and was not surprised to find Jacque walking a step behind her. She controlled the urge to run and calmly asked him "Did you want to talk? Can I help you?"

She was astonished to see plain hatred in his eyes. He stopped for a second and Alaska could sense the venom of his thoughts. They stood looking at each other for a few seconds in silence, and, then he walked away without saying a word. Alaska thought "Why? Why does he dislike me so much?"

That night, again she had the same dream. She heard someone screaming "Jacque". She jumped out of her bed sweating and feeling scared. She tried to remember her dream. She wanted to know who was screaming and who was Jacque, but could not remember and ended up with a throbbing headache. She promised herself that next time when she talked with Maxim she will ask him about Jacque and the screaming dream. Actually it had become a nightmare for her. She wondered at the significance of Jacque in her life.

Next day Maxim did call her. She was so happy to hear his voice that she forgot to tell him about her recurring nightmare. He asked her "Would you like to come for a seminar in Sedona sometime next month for a group of 'spiritual people'? It would be two days and one night trip for you. What do you think? Sometimes, the so called spiritual people are quite fixated and rigid in their opinion of spirituality. You will get a chance to learn more if they are like that."

Alaska said "Yes! But when? I have my exams coming up."

Maxim said "Give me the dates and I will pass it on to my school. They will work out when both of us can be available in Sedona. Princess, this one will be your fifth seminar with me. Don't forget you will be presenting the sixth one and I will be sitting with the audience."

Alaska groaned "You are making me nervous."

Maxim laughed and said "Remember, we are here to help people create happier lives for themselves. There is nothing to worry about. Your audience will love you, not because you are breathtakingly beautiful, but because you have the power to awaken them to their own power, their True-self, their inner magician."

Alaska murmured "Thank you."

"Cheer up Princess. It will be great fun, I assure you. Another thing- when would you like me to invite your friends for a meal?" Maxim asked.

"Invite my friends? Why?" Alaska asked surprised.

"Because they are your friends, and besides, you had said they wanted to meet me! Remember, they always missed me?" replied Maxim with a laugh.

"Yes, I know all three will come running to meet you, but you don't have to Maxim. I know you are busy. It is okay. You don't have to invite them." said Alaska.

"It is not okay Princess. I want to meet Julie, James and Mark because they are your friends. I want to know everyone who is, in some way, connected with you. So, I suggest, find out if they are available for dinner next Saturday." Maxim replied.

Alaska asked "Maxim, how do you remember their names? They will be thrilled. If you are sure, I will ask them and let you know. Where do I ask them to come for dinner?"

Maxim named a restaurant one of the best in town, at 7 PM. Alaska was feeling so happy she laughed out loud.

Maxim said "Share the joke."

Alaska replied "There is no joke. I am just happy, happy that I will see you next Saturday!"

"Princess, you made my day by saying that" said Maxim softly.

****

Alaska called her friends immediately. First she spoke with Julie and gave her Maxim's invitation.

Julie exclaimed "What? What did you say?"

Alaska laughed and said "Yes, you heard me. So, will you come for the dinner?"

Julie said "I cannot believe it. We have been trying to meet him for so long. Every time we are informed 'Mr. De Winter is not available', and now you say he is inviting us for dinner! Alaska, you bet I will be there. I will give anything to talk with Gladiator face-to-face. Aly, you are not kidding, are you?"

Alaska laughed and replied "No, Julie, I am not kidding. Gladiator did invite you three."

Julie thoughtfully asked "I wonder why he is inviting us? Why Alaska? Did you ask him to invite us?"

Alaska replied "No, I didn't. I had told him long back that you three would like to meet him. That is all."

Julie said "There is something you are not telling. Anyway, I am dying to meet Gladiator, I will be there. Thank you, Aly. Love you!"

Then she called James and then Mark. Their reaction to the dinner invitation was similar to that of Julie. First they couldn't believe it, and then they wanted to know the reason for the invitation. Anyway, both agreed and said they were looking forward to the evening with Gladiator.

Alaska sent an email to Maxim conveying their acceptance. She asked him if he could let her know his arrival time in Boston, she could come to De Winter Enterprises and meet him and his friend, Brian, at the same time. She had liked Brian. There was something good about him and she would like to meet him again.

She got a cryptic reply from Maxim saying "No need to come. I will see you at the restaurant on Saturday."

****

Brain was quite surprised to receive an invitation or was it an order, from Mr. De Winter, to join him for dinner in Boston this coming Saturday. In Boston? That means he travels from L.A. to Boston just for a dinner? There was no meeting or any conference scheduled for that Saturday. As the office had no idea about this dinner, he guessed it had to do something with Alaska, the beautiful Alaska, he couldn't forget. Hundreds of times he had asked himself why he couldn't have met Alaska before Maxim did. Just saying her name made him feel happy. But he kept his distance from her, because, he somehow knew that Alaska was someone very special in Maxim's life. Maxim had virtually shifted his main office from L.A. to Boston these past few months and Brian knew why. Brian debated what would be the best course of action. Should he go or should he not go. He thought of speaking with Maxim but finally succumbed to his desire to see Alaska again and accepted the invitation.

Alaska told her parents about the dinner. Her mother was surprised and asked "Does Gladiator often give such parties?"

Alaska replied "Honestly I don't know. He treats me to a burger or coffee when he is in town, but, so far I have not been to a party with him."

Alaska's mother asked her "What are you going to wear that evening?"

Alaska replied "Why? I didn't think about it. Should I wear something special?"

Her mother replied "The restaurant that Gladiator has invited you all to, may have a dinner dress code. Check it out and dress accordingly."

Alaska was excited that Maxim was coming after nearly a month, but at the same time she was a bit anxious about the whole thing.

In all the excitement about the dinner Alaska had forgotten to tell Maxim about her recurring night-mare. Anyway, she decided to tell him when he called next. But Maxim didn't call. Instead she got a call from Mr. Mendoza, from the taxi company, saying that he will be there at 7 PM to drive her to the restaurant. She felt disappointed. Anyway, as per her mother's suggestion, she wore a dark blue silky dress and piled up her hair to look mature.

Mr. Mendoza was there on time but surprisingly they met with heavy traffic en route to the restaurant. Just before they reached the restaurant, Mr. Mendoza got a call from Maxim. He told him they had arrived. Alaska felt more disappointed. Why didn't Maxim call her? She got out of the car and quickly ran up the few steps to the restaurant. As she entered the glass door, she saw Maxim, in black suit and tie, walking towards her with a gentle expression in his Indigo eyes. She forgot all her disappointments and walked straight into his arms. He hugged her and murmured "As enchanting as ever!" He looked at her for a moment, then, murmured softly "I thought, you wouldn't let me hug you in the presence of your friends!"

"My friends!" Alaska exclaimed and quickly stepped back. She saw Julie, James, Mark and Brian standing just behind Maxim, looking curiously at them. Alaska felt herself blushing. Maxim laughed and said "Let us go back to our table."

Alaska at last found her voice and asked her friends "When did you come?"

Julie replied "I didn't want to risk being late, so came half an hour ago."

Alaska looked at Brian and asked "Hi Brian, how are you? It is nice to meet you again."

Brian replied "It is a pleasure to meet you again Alaska. You are more breath-taking than I remembered you to be!"

Alaska was surprised to see Brian looking at her without blinking even once. There was a peculiar combination of joy and sadness in his brown eyes, which made her feel uncomfortable. She gently said "Thank you, Brian."

The waiter took their orders for drinks and appetizers. Alaska asked James "How have you been James? It has been ages since I saw you last. What have you been doing?"

They talked about their work till the drinks and appetizers arrived. Alaska looked up and saw Mark looking at her. She asked "Mark, why are you so silent?"

Mark slowly replied "It is amazing sitting with you and Gladiator. Your energies are palpable. I can feel your high vibrations. I know we are getting energized. I only hope I can meet you two in future as well."

Maxim said "Of course, you will. Any friend of Alaska will always be welcome at our place."

"Thank you. I will remember that Gladiator." Mark replied softly.

There was silence for a moment. Alaska didn't know what to say. Everyone was looking at her. James came to her rescue.

He said "Actually I had promised myself to thank you, Gladiator, for changing my life. So, thank you, thank you, thank you. I am grateful!"

After a moment he asked "Can we ask you some questions Gladiator or is it not the right time for Q and A?"

Maxim, without answering said "How is your mother James? Has she started playing piano again?"

James was astounded "How do you remember? Yes, my mother is better, better than she had been for decades. Thank you. And yes, she has started playing piano again."

Julie couldn't resist. She asked "Could I ask just one question? Please Gladiator?"

Hearing this Brian said "Maxim, I have never heard you speak as Gladiator. Give me the privilege of watching Gladiator in action. May be, then I will understand the un-explainable power of Mr. De Winter."

Maxim looked at Alaska. Everyone looked at her. Alaska quickly said "Yes, of course, please!"

Maxim said "Let us first enjoy our dinner. We can discuss whatever you want to discuss while having dessert and coffee."

Julie looked at Alaska with awe and murmured "Alaska, how does it feel?"

"What?" said Alaska and quickly changed the subject. She said "Julie, I like your dress. This peach shade suits you very much and with the pearl string you look very stylish."

Before the dinner was served Maxim said "I have just returned from Tokyo. I got little mementoes of Japan for you." Saying this Maxim took out several packages beautifully wrapped in multi colored papers and handed one to each one. He gave a square box to Alaska, but before she could look at it, he said "Come on Princess.

Let us Tango. I know this music that they are playing now. You will enjoy dancing to its beat."

Saying "Excuse me" to others, Maxim almost pulled Alaska out of her chair and headed to the dance floor. Several couples were already on the dance floor. The live band was good and lively.

Alaska quickly said "I am not a good dancer. I rarely dance and I don't know much about Tango."

Maxim didn't stop. When they were on the dance floor, he said "Nothing to it. Remain close and follow me. Dance as if no one is watching you. Let us have fun Princess. One ….two…..three" and they started. And after that they indeed had fun. Maxim moved fast from one end of the floor to the other, twirling, pulling and pushing Alaska. She couldn't stop giggling and laughing all the time. She was surprised to realize that Maxim, besides the energetic dancing, was also softly singing! She could only catch the last phrase of the song '…and then she came into my life'.

Finally when the lively music stopped, they stopped breathless and glowing. Alaska realized that they were the only dancers on the floor, others were standing in a circle around the floor, clapping and appreciating their performance. There was a demand for encore but Maxim moved off the floor saying "Thank you, but need water."

When they reached their table, Brian, Julie, James and Mark, who were earlier standing near the floor watching them dance, joined them at the table.

Brian said "Wow, that was some performance Maxim and Alaska! WOW! Maxim, wait till the media comes to know how you Tango."

Alaska, who was gulping water, said with a laugh "Maxim moved so fast, I held on to him for dear life! Whenever I thought I will trip over, he would lift me off the floor!"

James said "I haven't seen such beautiful, lively, well-coordinated Tango ever!"

Maxim smiled and said "Thank you. Do you know that Tango is not just a dance? It is poetry, poetry set in music, with fast foot-work, full of emotion and is a physical expression of an un-expressed passion."

Mark softly said "You two were great! Your dancing was out of this world. Look around. Everyone is looking at you two!"

Alaska piped in "Mark, wherever Maxim goes, people stare at him. It doesn't bother him. He is oblivious to it."

Maxim, who was sipping water, said with a laugh "Princess, it is time you learned to share the blame. If people are staring, I am not alone to blame." After a moment he added "I see you have not opened your gifts. Please do."

Everyone reached for their gift and removed the wrapper to find Japanese scroll made of golden colored satin with a little message written in the center. James read his scroll. It said "Know thy power and it will set you free"

Mark's scroll read "Love is the final frontier"

Brian's scroll read "Befriend the inner magician to have a miraculous life"

Julie opened her scroll and read "When you love, you become divine"

There was silence around the table. Everyone was touched by Maxim's thoughtfulness.

Maxim softly prompted Alaska "Open your box Princess."

Hearing Maxim's voice, everyone thanked him for the gift. Julie said to Alaska "Aly, open your gift and show us."

Alaska slowly opened her square box to reveal a five string pearl necklace with an intricately designed diamond clasp on the left shoulder. Seeing it, Julie exclaimed "Oh, it is gorgeous. It must have cost you the Earth!"

Maxim said "Won't you put it on Princess? I want to see if it looks as good as I thought it would."

Alaska felt over conscious with everyone looking at her. She put it on and heard 'oh Wow' 'Beautiful' from her friends. Alaska touched her necklace and asked Maxim "Are these very expensive Maxim?"

Maxim, without replying her, looked at her for a long moment and finally said with a smile "Beautiful."

Brian came to her rescue and said "Alaska, don't give it a thought. This man is too rich. He can easily afford ten of them!"

Alaska, with a desire to change the topic, quickly said "Hey, where is my note, my message?"

Maxim replied "It is there in the box." Julie found the note and said "Yes, I found it." She read it "Read me, if you can."

Julie looked surprised but Alaska said "OK, but don't give me complicated sentences or scenes to describe."

Alaska slightly turned towards Maxim and said "OK, I am ready." Brian, Mark, James and Julie silently looked on, very curious and very interested to know the outcome.

After a few moments, Alaska mumbled and said "No, I don't get it. Try something else."

Maxim laughed and said "Ok. What about this?"

After a few seconds, Alaska complained "Aren't you choosing difficult scenes Maxim?"

Julie and James both said "Alaska tell what you read. We are dying of curiosity. If it is wrong, Gladiator will correct you."

Alaska said "OK, I think Maxim said –Radiate love, the world is starved."

Mark asked "Is that right Gladiator?"

Maxim replied "Yes, it is."

Brian said "OK, so Alaska could read the second message. I am curious. Please try to read the first one."

Alaska saw Maxim grinning at her. She said "OK, Brian, for you, I will try to read the first one. I think he said – I was like air, free, free to roam the universe. Now I am….. enchanted, …..enslaved, and…and….I lost my freedom."

Brian asked "Maxim?"

Maxim replied with a mischievous smile "That is true."

Julie said "Oh my God! That means you two can talk anywhere without others having any knowledge of it!"

James asked "Can you read anybody Gladiator?"

Maxim replied "If I wanted to, yes, but I don't! I am not interested in others, so why should I waste my time reading them?"

Brian said in awe "Maxim, you make a deadly opponent. I feel sorry for people who think they can out-smart you. OK, Boss, you got another student for your spiritual school."

Maxim said "Good. Please remember telepathy, intuition, teleporting, bi-locating etc. are our natural inherent powers. We are born with it! Believe it! All you need is a little practice my friends. Don't try it, just do it!"

The dinner was served and they got busy enjoying the food. It was exceptionally good. Now the ambience of the place had changed with dimmed light and soft, soothing music.

Alaska looked across the table and found Maxim looking at her with a gentle expression in his Indigo eyes. She smiled and wished they were alone. She got an instant reply from Maxim "Your wish is my command princess. Should we leave our friends to finish their meal on their own or, better still, should we ask them to leave us alone to have our two-some dinner?"

The whole idea was so ridiculous Alaska couldn't stop giggling, imagining the two scenes that could follow the two options. Everyone looked at her suspiciously. She tried to control but she couldn't stop laughing out loud, especially, when Maxim joined her laughter. After few moments Maxim said "The evening has been great, thanks to you four. Someday I will share the joke, but if we appear rude, please forgive me. I am the culprit."

After the dinner plates were removed and dessert with coffee was served, Maxim reminded Alaska's friends "You had some questions."

Julie looked at James and Mark and asked "Can I go first?"

When they agreed, Julie said "Gladiator, my dream was to become a doctor and thanks to you, I am on my way to becoming one. I am grateful to you for that. My question is why I cannot manifest my other desires?"

Maxim said "Julie, I take it for granted that you know the process of manifesting your desire. You undoubtedly believe that you, and only you, create your reality. There is no limiting belief contradicting this knowledge what so ever in your mind."

Julie replied "Yes, I know and that is why I don't understand why I cannot manifest my other desires."

Maxim asked "Did you know that a dream is a desire that you love?"

There was silence on the table. After thinking for some time Julie said "I don't understand."

Maxim replied "You can have endless list of desires arising from your ego mind and desires of your family, friends or society that you feel obliged to try and achieve. Pay attention to your feeling for your desire. Julie, whose desire are you chasing – your own or someone else's? Does this desire ignite you, set you on fire? If not, let it go."

Maxim paused and waited for Julie to say something. After some time Julie said "Do you mean to say that I should try to manifest my one dream and forget the rest?"

Maxim replied "If you can manifest your one true desire, the rest will be taken care of. You do not have to struggle for them. But, in case, you have a desire that you definitely want to manifest, you will need to love it."

Maxim paused. Julie asked him "How?"

Maxim smiled and asked "Don't you love someone, something, some memory, may be a beautiful sunrise, ocean waves, or the round shiny eyes of a baby?"

Julie replied "I think so."

Maxim said "Well, then, use that memory as a trigger to awaken love in your heart and body, for your new desire. It will take some practice but it is doable. Once you start feeling love and excitement for your new desire, you have transformed an ordinary desire to the status of a 'dream' Julie!"

Julie Looked at Maxim with awe. She asked "How come you have answer to every question? How come you are so attractive, so rich and all good things rolled into one?"

Maxim laughed and said "Alaska doesn't think so."

Julie asked surprised "She doesn't? What does she think?"

Alaska groaned and said "Oh no, I didn't say that."

Maxim laughed and continued "I am Gladiator to her when I am talking about spirituality. I become Maxim when I treat her to burger and French fries, and, I, alas, become that awful Mr. De Winter when I am at the Enterprises' office because, she thinks, there, I transform into an obnoxious billionaire."

Julie was aghast at this description. Others laughed. Alaska knew everyone was enjoying except Mark who was looking at her with a kind of sad, nostalgic expression. She smiled and Mark smiled back but his expression didn't change. She felt sad. She wondered why she couldn't love him. He was such a nice person. In the next moment she got her answer "Because you cannot love everyone who loves you Princess!"

She found Maxim looking at her unwaveringly. She heard him say "Radiate love equally just as Sun bestows its warmth on all."

She nodded her head and asked her friends "Anyone for more coffee? I am going to have."

Finally everyone had a second cup of coffee.

Maxim asked "Was there any other question? Mark?"

Mark replied "No. Actually I learn more just by listening to you, and surprisingly you always answer the question dearest to my heart."

James asked "Can I ask you something?"

Maxim said "Sure."

James said "You told Julie a 'dream' is a desire that you love, but what is this love you talk about?"

Maxim said "The love I talk about is not the physical expression of it. The love I talk about is beyond physical. It pervades the whole creation as it is the building block of our universe. Love is the divine force of creation itself, and in the absence of this eternal vibration of our Creator, creation cannot take place. When humanity gets disconnected from this divine stream of love, it faces a period of conflict, destruction, war and un-told misery."

Maxim paused for a moment and asked "James?"

James said in wonder "You mean the omniscient, omnipresent and omnipotent God is love and we need to vibrate at the frequency of love to become awake to this divine Force?"

Maxim smiled and said "Yes, you got it James!"

There was complete silence. Everyone was trying to absorb this information in their own way.

Julie asked "Gladiator, could you please tell us some simple and easy ways to connect with this divine force you call 'love?"

Maxim smiled and looked at Alaska and asked "Princess, can you help us?"

Alaska thought for some time and then said "I think the easiest way to connect with any divine force is, to use the vibration of the word 'love' itself Maxim."

Julie immediately asked "How?"

Alaska replied "By using the word 'love' repeatedly like a mantra! OK, Julie, this is one of the ways you can do it- sit with your spine straight and start breathing slowly and deeply. When you are completely relaxed and calm, say, out loud or silently, I….love…. you, I…love…you, I…..love…..you, to yourself. If you prefer, you can use a mirror and look into your eyes while saying it. Be present in your body. This practice raises your frequency, and as you keep on doing it, you will connect with the eternal stream of divine love."

Alaska paused for a second, then continued "Instead of saying 'I love you', you can also say 'I love myself' or 'I am love', if you prefer. Keep repeating it till you feel the shift in your vibration."

Alaska stopped and Maxim took over. He said "I must warn you the effects, of these three statements, are quite different from one another on your physical system. Experiment with all three statements and choose the one which feels best."

Alaska looked at Maxim and asked "Is there any other simple practice using the word 'love' Maxim?"

Maxim smiled and asked "Would you like to demonstrate one for your friends?"

Alaska said "OK, what do I have to do?"

Maxim said "This practice can be done only with a friend or a partner. This is very powerful, if done correctly, and the shift is almost immediate."

Maxim continued "Princess turn towards me and look into my eyes and repeat whatever I say."

Alaska said "OK".

Maxim smiled and looked deep into her eyes and said "Princess?"

Alaska surprised said "Hmm?"

Maxim said slowly "I...love...you."

For a second Alaska didn't get it, then she remembered she had to repeat. She looked into Maxim's Indigo eyes and slowly repeated "I...love...you."

At the beginning they were smiling while repeating 'I love you', but soon everyone could see they had stopped smiling while, unwaveringly looking into others eyes. Mark, who was sensitive to energy, could feel their high vibrations. Brian, James and Julie could also sense the difference in the air around them. They silently looked on in awe.

Then they heard Maxim say to Alaska "Relax and close your eyes."

And with that everyone relaxed but soon they were startled to hear Maxim say sharply "Breathe Princess! Open your eyes, now!" He was out of his chair and half way round the table when Alaska gingerly mumbled "Must you scream?"

Maxim stood there keenly looking at Alaska. When she opened her eyes, he smiled and returned to his chair.

James asked "What happened?"

Maxim replied "Nothing much, except she forgot to breathe."

Brian looked concerned and asked "Isn't that dangerous?"

Maxim replied "If she doesn't breathe for long, then yes, she can damage her physical system, especially her brain, depriving it of oxygen."

Brian asked "If you were not here Maxim, what would have happened to her? You wouldn't know that she had stopped breathing!"

Maxim softly murmured "I always know if she is in any kind of danger or pain. I can shout her awake."

Mark looked worried and asked "And if she doesn't hear you?"

Maxim smiled and said "Then I will have to physically come and shake her awake! Don't worry, Mark, I won't let anything hurt your friend."

Mark immediately said "I don't doubt you or your immense powers, Gladiator. I was curious."

Julie asked "What do you mean by physically come? Bi-locate? Can you do it in seconds?"

Maxim said "Yes, if need be."

Alaska was feeling miserable with all these questions and said "Forgive me but haven't we digressed from our main topic of discussion- how to connect with the divine force of love simply by meditating on the word 'love'?"

Maxim smiled and said "Yes, we have. I trust you will use it to make your life extra-ordinary my friends."

Julie said "I realized today that you two are too advanced for me. I feel overwhelmed. The knowledge that you impart so casually, Gladiator, is beyond my understanding. I am grateful to you and will always remain so for transforming my life but I don't think I can ever become your ultimate magician, Gladiator."

Maxim said gently "Julie, you don't have to become, because you already are! You are born with it! You are born with the power to create anything you desire. In truth you are giving the Creation its creation! Anything that I can do, you can do it too! Believe it Julie."

James said "Gladiator, my meeting with you completely changed my life. Miracles happened. I know it was your power, but, as you say we too have the same power, then I hope one day I will be able

124

to help others as you do. And guess what- very soon I am going to return the money you payed for my loan."

Maxim said "That is good but do not return it to me, instead pay it forward. Give it to another student who needs it with the instruction that he/she should pay it forward when he/she has earned enough money to do so."

Mark said "Now, I guess, it is my turn to say thank you to you Gladiator but I cannot find the right words. Somehow you did change us into the best version of ourselves. You disrupted our mediocre lives and pushed us to achieve our dreams. Thank you. If ever I can be of any service to you, just call me. I will do anything for you two."

Maxim gently said "Thank you Mark. I will remember that."

Mark asked "Gladiator, why don't you ever accept the fact that you are a great teacher, a healer and that you have access to immense power to change or transform anything?"

Maxim replied with a smile "If I accept that, there will be long queues of people waiting to be 'healed' every day. And after a few days they will be back in the queue because they would have had time to create new, so called, problems! This cycle will go on endlessly. Mark, what I want is, make every human aware of the inherent power they were born with, so that they never ask or beg again for anything and they take their rightful place as gods, as creators of this wonderful creation! Does it answer your question Mark? I want people to learn to fish for themselves instead of giving them a fish to eat."

Mark conceded "Yes, that makes sense."

Maxim looked at Alaska and others and asked "Are you ready to go? Shall we?"

They moved towards the door. Thanks and good byes were said. Maxim, Brian and Alaska let others leave first. When they were alone waiting for their cars, Brian asked Maxim "Was this party a celebration?"

Maxim smiled and replied "It always is a celebration when Princess is around."

Brian persisted "No announcement?"

Maxim laughed and said "Patience Brian!"

Brian said "I just wondered. Do let me know."

Alaska asked "What are you two talking about?"

Brian said "It was a great evening Alaska. I saw a different side of Maxim tonight. Alaska, you simply radiate a rare combination of friendship and joy that no one can miss. I only wish I had met you earlier. If ever you need something, call me Alaska. I will do anything for you." Saying this he quickly went down the steps to open the car door for her. She got in and said "You are very kind Brian. Thank you."

Maxim looked at Alaska as he put the Lamborghini in gear. He asked "Tired? Sleepy?"

Alaska replied absentmindedly "No, not really."

Maxim asked "Thinking of what Brian said?"

Alaska nodded her head and asked "Why did he say that Maxim?"

"Time will tell." Maxim gently replied.

"In ten minutes we shall be at your campus, so start sharing all the news now." Maxim prompted her.

Alaska said "Oh, I had to tell you so many things......, but first, thank you Maxim for inviting my friends for dinner. You made their day, or their lives, as they keep saying, and thank you for the gifts. When did you find time to buy the gifts and write the little notes? You are so thoughtful Maxim."

She hugged his arm and looked up at him and said "Thank you for being you Maxim."

Maxim murmured "I won't be able to drive if you keep saying things like that."

Alaska grinned and Maxim said "Alright, now tell me when I can meet your parents. This month won't be possible, so choose a weekend next month."

Alaska asked "But, why do you want to meet my parents?"

Maxim replied "Because they are your parents, they love you and you love them!"

"But, why do you have to meet them?" asked Alaska.

Maxim laughed and said "OK, now you tell me why you don't want me to meet your parents. Whenever I ask, you avoid. Why? Do you think they may ask me questions that I may not be able to answer? You must have a very low opinion of my intelligence!"

Alaska smiled and said "No, I don't. My parents think very highly of you, of Gladiator but…"

Maxim asked "But what"

Alaska said "I don't know. My Mom asks how you are as a person…."

Maxim asked "And what do you tell her?"

Alaska said "The truth."

Maxim asked "And that is….?"

Alaska replied "that you are kind, gentle, and considerate….. but, I know, my answer doesn't satisfy her. Even Dad sometime seems worried, I am not sure why."

They had reached the campus.

Maxim said "Choose the weekend that suits you. I have to meet them soon. I promise you my answer will satisfy them."

Alaska half-heartedly said "Really?"

Maxim laughed and said "Really. Trust me. Why don't you give me their telephone number? I will call them and fix a date."

"No, I will do it." said Alaska.

"Don't postpone any further, will you?" asked Maxim.

Alaska replied "No, I won't. Maxim I wanted to tell you about Jacque."

Maxim asked "What happened? Still staring at you?"

Alaska said "That he does, but I am scared of my night-mares. I see a woman falling down a cliff screaming 'Jacque'. It makes me feel very uncomfortable and I cannot fall asleep after that."

Maxim asked "Can you see her face?"

"No, I always see her from the back. I also see a crowd of people down-below shouting, cheering or something….." replied Alaska.

Maxim was silent for some time, and then he said "If it happens again, remember me."

"Remember you? What do you mean?" asked Alaska.

Maxim turned to look at Alaska. He gently ran his fingers through her hair and said "Jacque and Maxim cannot be present at the same time. If you call Maxim, Jacque will leave."

Alaska asked curiously "Why? What do you mean?"

"You will soon know. It is quite late. Go and sleep now. I have to be up early to catch my morning flight. I will let you know about the Sedona seminar soon. Take care, my precious Princess." said Maxim.

Alaska, with a sigh, got out of the car and stood on the curb waving to Maxim with a smile on her face but her heart was silently saying "I don't want you to go" and she heard "and I don't want to leave you ever! We will remedy that soon Princess."

She saw Maxim wave once from inside the car and then he was gone.

CHAPTER 11

Alaska was on the train going back to Boston after spending the weekend with her parents. She had really enjoyed the trip. Her parents, as loving as ever, had pampered her. Mom had prepared all her favorite food. They had asked about the seminars in Alaska and on board the cruise in the Caribbean. She had loved giving them all the details of the seminars. She told them about the island they had visited. The only discordant note was the question – how was Gladiator as a person. She had said he was always kind, gentle and very considerate, but she knew, her answer didn't satisfy them. She had shown the pearl necklace that Maxim had got for her from Japan. Her mother had said it looked expensive and had asked her if he got gifts for her friends too and she had said yes he did.

Later she had told them about the seminar in Sedona with the spiritual group. Maxim wanted her to attend this seminar because he said seminars with the so called spiritual groups were unique and quite interesting, and it will give her ample opportunity to learn how to deal with such groups.

Then her mother had told Alaska that soon they were expecting another holographic presentation from Gladiator at their club. She had surprised Alaska by asking her if she thought Gladiator would personally come again for a presentation at the club.

Involuntarily Alaska had said "Oh Mom, Maxim wants to come and meet you two. He has been asking me to find a weekend suitable to you."

Her parents were utterly surprised and had asked her "Is he planning another presentation here?"

And Alaska had replied reluctantly "No, not for a presentation. Maxim wants to come here only to meet you."

Her mother had asked "What? Gladiator wants to meet us and you never told us? What is wrong Aly? Tell him to come whenever he can. It will be suitable for us."

Even her Dad had looked perplexed and had asked her "Why didn't you tell us little one? You know how much we appreciate and respect Gladiator."

And she had mumbled "You don't know how busy he is Dad. He is just being kind and considerate as usual."

"Did you ask him why he wanted to meet us?" Her Dad had asked.

She had replied "Yes, I did. He says because they are your parents and they love you and you love them."

Her parents had looked at each other. Then Dad had said "Please tell him we are eagerly looking forward to his visit. Just let us know the date. Any date that suits him is acceptable to us. Little one don't you know how we would love to meet him? But how will you tell him? Do you telephone him?"

She had replied "No, I don't because he is always travelling to different parts of the world with different time zones. Maxim calls me, usually at night. I will tell him then."

After a short pause her Dad had asked her "Little one, you don't seem happy. You don't want him to meet us? Do you?"

She had answered "Dad, he is a very kind and very caring person. I don't want you or Mom to ask him questions that might upset him."

Dad had assured her "Relax, we will not ask him anything that might upset your friend. But little one, aren't you forgetting something? He is a friend to you, Maxim to you, but he is also the Gladiator to the world! He answers thousands of questions put to him from all across the world without a second's hesitation. How do you think we can possibly upset him?"

Her mother had quickly added "Don't worry Aly. I will not ask him anything. Just let him come. You don't know how happy I am that Gladiator wants to meet us."

Alaska smiled as she remembered the surprised look on her parents faces when she had announced her decision to join Gladiator's spiritual school in L.A. after completing her Masters. She had also told them her plans to do Ph.D. and that she had already started doing some research on the subject.

Her father had said "You are really moving fast Little-one. What are you researching at the moment?"

She had said "Theory of multi-verses, certain galaxies and stars. Maxim has already done it but wants to confirm if his experiences could be replicated."

Dad had asked "Experiences?"

She had tried to explain "Our research is in actually connecting or communicating with higher intelligences, much advanced civilizations, beyond physical realm. They vibrate at very high frequencies and so, communicating with them is an art we have to learn. Dad, they want humanity to progress. They are ready to assist us but the problem is humans do not understand them. To overcome this problem, Maxim is opening a channel, so to speak, so that others could easily communicate with higher intelligences and benefit from their immense knowledge to live happier lives."

Her mother, who had been listening, looked worried and had asked "Is it safe to communicate with them Aly?"

She had replied "Mom, I am safe, because whenever I communicate with them, Maxim is with me. He never leaves me alone with them. Mom you worry because you don't know how caring Maxim is!"

After a few seconds her Dad had gently asked "Little-one, you love him?"

Alaska had replied truthfully "I don't know Dad. I only know I am happy because Maxim is in my world."

Dad had smiled and said "That is it, Little-one!"

CHAPTER 12

Alaska was so excited she could hardly close her eyes. She looked at the clock. It was nearly mid-night. She had to catch the early morning flight to Phoenix for the Sedona seminar. Maxim had told her Mr. Mendoza would be there to take her to the airport. Alaska quickly closed her eyes with a smile on her lips. Before she fell asleep she heard Maxim laughing and saying "Sleep. See you soon Princess."

Next she knew was her alarm ringing. She jumped out of her bed, quickly got ready and walked out with her small carry-on suitcase to find Mr. Mendoza waiting for her. He was always happy to see her and always welcomed her with a big smile. They drove to the airport and now Alaska was on the flight to Phoenix. Maxim had suggested that she sleep for a couple of hours on the flight and rest before the long evening seminar in Sedona. The wide seat that turned into a flat bed, was quite inviting but she was too happy to sleep. She enjoyed the sumptuous breakfast. After the breakfast she was wondering what she could do to avoid having to chat with the lady sitting next to her and the business executive sitting across the aisle, who seemed very interested in her. She took out her notepad to record her impression of the spiritual group they were going to address this evening, but that did not deter the lady from asking her endless questions. Alaska heard Maxim laugh and say "Close your eyes and sleep." So, she did close her eyes and dozed for some time.

Flight had landed in Phoenix on time. Alaska had just entered the arrival hall pulling her little suitcase. She stood looking for Maxim. After a moment she saw him standing surrounded by some people. He saw her at the same time and started walking towards her. She, as usual, ran straight into his arms.

He hugged her and said "It feels great to have you in my arms, Princess. You have made me more physical than I thought I was."

Alaska looked into his eyes with a big grin when she remembered her father saying "That is it, Little-one!"

For a moment she stood looking at Maxim without saying a word.

Maxim gently asked "Seen a ghost or did your favorite Indigo eyes turned green?"

She quickly looked away and asked "Who were the people you were talking to just now?"

Maxim smiled and murmured "Faint of heart."

When Alaska didn't look or say anything Maxim replied "They are part of the spiritual group we are meeting this evening."

Maxim keenly looked at Alaska and asked her "Would you like to eat something before we drive to Sedona?"

"No, let us go now" said Alaska, and now they were on way to Sedona. Maxim tried to ask her about her parents, her classes, but she answered in monosyllables. After that there was silence in the car.

Alaska suddenly realized that Maxim had taken the exit from the highway. She asked "Where are you going?"

Without replying her, Maxim drove to the nearest parking lot and stopped the car. He released his seat-belt and turned towards Alaska and said "Look at me Princess. I thought you liked to look into my Indigo eyes."

Alaska softly said without looking at him "Yes."

"Then why don't you look at me now?" asked Maxim. He took her chin and turned her face towards him and said "Looking at me won't make any difference. Even if you were thousands of miles away from me, I will know your feelings, so don't try to hide from me. Tell me one thing – are you angry with yourself for caring for me?"

Alaska shyly said "No! I thought it will make you feel uncomfortable if you knew that I…that I cared for you."

Maxim looked at her with a gentle smile for a long moment and then said "Uncomfortable? No! I am thrilled. I am excited. I am happy beyond words, that at last, at long last, you have become aware of me as a man instead of always thinking of me as Gladiator, the spiritual teacher!"

Alaska shyly peeped at him and asked "Really Maxim?"

Maxim ran his fingers through her hair and said "Really, Princess! You don't need to ask, you can read me."

Alaska at last looked into his eyes and nodded her head. Maxim laughed and asked "Now that we have stopped, we can as well pick up some coffee. What do you say?"

"Yes, but we have to hurry. You said it will take us two hours to reach Sedona, didn't you?" asked Alaska with her usual dazzling smile.

After that, they shared news while driving to Sedona, as they always did. Alaska was happy to hear that soon De Winter Enterprises was going to acquire the island in the Caribbean that they had visited while on the cruise.

He said "Do you remember the entrepreneur group from the cruise? Well, the guy called Brian is very keen to meet you. He has asked for an appointment with me but I know he hopes to see you there. Poor guy!"

Maxim asked her "Did you tell your parents that I will be visiting them on the 26th?"

Alaska said "No, I haven't told them the date."

Maxim laughed and said "Still not comfortable with the idea, are you?"

Alaska said "I don't know why you want to meet them."

Maxim glanced at her and gently said "I have already told you why. Relax, Princess, my answer will satisfy your parents. Trust me."

After a moment he asked "What about your night-mare? Still get them?"

Alaska said "Yes, I do, but as you had told me, I immediately think of you and feel better. But why do I have them Maxim? My hairs stand on end when I hear the woman scream 'Jacque'."

After a short silence Maxim asked "Did you check the vibes for the evening seminar?"

Alaska replied "They seem eager to meet you but at the same time critical of you. I really didn't understand their vibes. What do you think Maxim?"

Maxim replied "It is going to be an interesting evening, one way or the other."

Soon they were at the resort. They checked in and then went to the coffee shop to find something to eat. They didn't have much time as the seminar was scheduled to start at 5 PM. They were busy eating when a group of people approached them. Alaska was surprised to hear one of them ask "You are Gladiator, aren't you?"

Maxim responded easily "Well, some people do prefer to address me as Gladiator." He carried on eating unconcerned. Alaska followed suit. The lady who had asked the question said "We have come to Sedona just to listen to you. Hope the seminar is as good as it is reputed to be."

Maxim replied easily "Well, you will have to wait for a few hours to know for sure."

The lady asked "Could you tell us what subjects you would be covering this evening."

Maxim smiled and said "No, I cannot do that."

Alaska saw the lady bristling at the answer. She sounded annoyed when she asked "What do you mean? Is it a secret?"

Maxim easily replied while continuing to eat "No, it is not a secret but it depends on the audience. I tell them what they need to hear. So, I am unable to enlighten you at the moment as I myself don't know what it is going to be."

The lady sounded angry. She asked "You mean you don't come prepared for the seminar?"

Maxim replied with a smile "I never prepare. Sorry to disappoint you."

He looked at Alaska and asked "Finished? Ready to go?"

Alaska nodded and got up to go when the lady asked "Is she your assistant? Will she be speaking too?"

Maxim smiled and said "No, she is my friend. She may talk if she wants to."

Saying this he guided Alaska out of the coffee shop. When they were in the elevator, Alaska asked "Why was the lady angry and rude?"

Maxim replied "People get angry and rude when they are not happy within and most common reason for being unhappy is they are disconnected from their True-self. Every heart wants to be validated, to be loved and to be cherished as only their True-self can do. But they are looking for it outside of themselves. They, of course, cannot find it there, so they blame someone or something for this feeling of lack and that gives them a temporary satisfaction. The seminar should help her."

By now they had reached their rooms. They went in to get ready for the seminar. Alaska wore the new sea-green chiffon dress that Mom had bought for her for the seminar. She had insisted that Alaska wore the pearl necklace that Maxim had brought from Japan with the dress. She looked in the long mirror. It looked good but she wondered if she would look over-dressed.

After she was ready, she called her parents and told them she had reached Sedona. They wanted to know if Maxim was there to receive her at the Phoenix airport. She gave them all the news and added at the end "Maxim would be coming over to meet you on Saturday the 26th next month."

Her parents were very pleased. Her mother started planning menu for lunch.

Alaska said "Mom, I don't know when he will arrive. May be he will come in the evening."

Her mother said "Then I will prepare the best dinner possible for him."

Alaska said "OK Mom, whatever. It is time for the seminar. I have to go. Bye Mom." Saying this she opened her door to find Maxim waiting for her looking as handsome as ever.

She impishly said "Hi handsome!"

Maxim said "I am blessed that you spared a glance at this non-entity and found him handsome."

Alaska giggled and said "But people do find this non-entity so attractive that they can hardly take their eyes off him!"

Maxim laughed and said "But you do, don't you? Did you look in the mirror before you opened the door?"

Alaska said "Oh, no. Am I over-dressed? Should I take off the necklace?"

Maxim said "No, you will not. I am feeling sorry that I didn't get a crown for you to go with the necklace. You look a fairy princess. People will find it difficult to take their eyes off you tonight. I will have to keep a strong watch lest a prince charming takes you away."

Alaska laughed and asked Maxim "Do I sit with the audience tonight?"

Maxim replied "No, you don't. You sit on the stage where I can keep an eye on you."

As they had already reached the auditorium Alaska couldn't ask him why. There was a huge poster by the main door announcing the evening seminar with Gladiator's portrait covering half of it. His piercing Indigo eyes in the portrait startled everyone entering the auditorium.

Alaska stopped to look and appreciate the picture.

Maxim murmured "I don't like it, but, I suppose, the host thinks people have to know the messenger before they can get the message."

They were received by the group leader. Maxim introduced Alaska and asked for a chair for her on the stage.

Then Maxim was formally introduced as Gladiator and the welcome speech was read. As usual, after the speech, he stood silently for nearly a minute looking at his audience with a gentle smile. Alaska wondered why the group had invited Maxim if they did not agree with his views on spirituality.

Then she saw Maxim waving to the audience. He began easily "Good evening friends. I feel honored to be invited to speak at such an elite gathering. I understand you have some questions for me. Please go ahead."

A lady from the front row said "Your formula, 'dream, then follow your dream', does not work for me. What do you have to say?"

Maxim smiled and said "Universal laws always work. Even at this very moment you are creating, you are creating what you prefer, what you focus on and it will manifest as your other desires have done in the past. It is a flawed notion that Universal laws work for some and do not work for others. A common reason why people stop manifesting their desires/dreams is that they start resisting change in their lives. You are comfortable with your old beliefs. You like to follow your old routine, habits, behavior, and life-style. Your life is on auto-pilot, run by your subconscious. You are in your comfort zone. Your body and mind will resist change. So, if you have a dream and you want a different life, you need to change something in yourself. Change your beliefs, change your self-image, change your habits and rest assured, you will create the life of your dreams! If you cannot make yourself change, then you will go on recreating your past in your future. As the Seers have said you have to die to your old-self my friend before you can be born anew!"

Maxim stopped and looked at the lady who had said your formula does not work for me. He gave her time to ask further questions, but she didn't. Alaska smiled. She knew when Gladiator spoke people didn't talk, they just listened. She remembered when Maxim had come to her university for the first time, a lot of people used to say that he mesmerizes his audience.

After a short pause Maxim asked "Any other question?"

Again a lady got up and asked "Do you believe in God?"

Maxim smiled and replied "It depends on what you mean by God. You will first have to explain the meaning that you assign to the word 'god', before I can truthfully answer your question."

As Maxim paused, he saw a man sitting quite far back in the hall, frantically waving his arms. A mike was sent to him and he said "I am Jeffry. I have come from Texas to see Gladiator because my friend said Gladiator can solve my problem."

Maxim asked "How can Gladiator help you Jeffry?"

Jeffry asked "Are you the Gladiator?"

Maxim smiled and replied "People call me Gladiator. How can I help you?"

Jeffry said "I warn you my question has nothing to do with spirituality. Can you still help?"

Maxim said "You are a spiritual being, and so anything to do with you has to be spiritual. Anyway, you are welcome to tell me the cause of your un-ease."

Jeffry said with disgust "It is that damned 'love'."

After a little pause he asked "Should I continue? Can you help?"

Maxim replied with a smile "Sure. We need to know how 'love' became 'that damned love'."

Jeffrey began in a rush "OK. It is about a slip of a girl. She came to our neighborhood as a toddler, who walked straight to me and caught hold of my hand with her chubby little hands sticky with chocolate. Her father died of cancer. Her mother had no time for the little girl and one day just walked off. My mother took care of her and when she passed away, it became my duty to take care of her. I sent her to school and then to college. I took her to the doctor when she was not well, man, I did everything for her that a good guardian should do. And, now, she tells me she has got a job in the city. And, so, she will be moving to the city, living alone there, which is three hour drive from my ranch. How can I keep an eye on her? I can't keep driving for six hours daily to look after her. But she is not ready to listen. She keeps saying 'what difference does it make to you. You don't love me!' I told her she should stay with me and do her Masters as her professor says she is very smart. But, no sir, she will go to the city and earn money to repay me for her up-keep. God knows, I am rich enough to feed five more families without feeling the pinch! I don't know how to make her stay. She always comes up with 'why bother, you don't love me'. Tell me Gladiator, how does one love? Anyway what is this damned love she keeps talking about?"

Gladiator said with a smile "Ah, so we come back to the 'damned love'. Before we talk about how to love, let us give you some idea what love is."

Maxim looked at Alaska and said "Princess, could you please help our friend Jeffrey to understand what love is?"

Alaska didn't want to talk to a person who kept cursing 'love' but she didn't want to refuse Maxim, so she got up with the mike. She tried to see Jeffrey, but he was sitting so far back from the stage she could not. She closed her eyes and tried to read his vibration. She was pleasantly surprised to find an open hearted kind man there.

With a happy smile she began "Love is many splendored things. Have you heard that Jeffrey? It is true. It is not one thing. It is all inclusive, all embracing divine energy of creation. Love endows you with divinity. You cannot control it with logic or reason still every heart craves it. Do you know why? Because love is our very essence! We are made out of the energy that is vibrating at the frequency of love. We are like that fish which wants to know what water is. We live in this divine stream of love and still don't know what love is. Love is the essential nature of the Creator. Jeffrey I hope you understand now the importance of this energy, this emotion called love. Love is divine, it can never be damned!"

Alaska paused. She wanted to give Jeffrey time to digest this information.

After some time Jeffrey asked her sounding quite perplexed "So, how does one know if one loves someone?"

Alaska replied "Well, you feel happy, you feel alive in her/his presence. Emotion of love is something that ignites you from within.

You want to be with her/him all the time for no obvious reason to do so. Does it make sense Jeffrey?"

Jeffrey replied in a gruff voice "Yes. I think I understand."

Alaska continued "There is another point to be noted. If you truly love someone, you allow her/him to remain as she/he is. You don't expect her to change or improve to please you. It is like a classical painting. You don't go with paint and brush and put a stroke here and a stroke there to improve the painting. You let it be! She is perfect in your eyes as she is, otherwise you wouldn't love her and cherish her!"

Alaska paused. Maxim softly said "Well said Princess."

Alaska smiled at him and continued "Jeffrey, is it clear to you now? Do you know what you feel for your …slip of a girl? Do you know what you need to say to her?"

Jeffrey gruffly said "Yes and no. Yes, I know what I feel for her. No, I don't know what to say to her."

Alaska thought for a second and said "What about this. You could say 'I love you more than anyone in the world', or, 'I love you beyond reason', and 'Will you marry me?'"

Jeffrey immediately said "Marry? I cannot marry her. She is twelve years younger to me. How can I ask her to marry me?"

Alaska smiled and said "just too bad then!"

Jeffrey said "What? What do you mean by that?"

Maxim got up and said "It means you have to convince her of your love, that is, of course, if you love her. It appears Jeffrey, without you being aware, she has been holding your heart in her little sticky hands. She made her choice as a toddler but you have been blind to it. It is time for you to openly lay your claim."

"But how? What do I say?" asked Jeffrey.

"Exactly what this lady told you a minute ago!" said Maxim.

Maxim looked at Alaska and said "I love you more than anyone in the world."

Alaska nodded. Maxim continued "I love you beyond reason." Maxim looked at Alaska for confirmation. Alaska again nodded.

Then he said "Will you marry me? Alaska said "yes" and nodded in agreement. Suddenly Alaska realized what she had said and felt foolish. She looked at Maxim who was softly laughing with a teasing expression in his Indigo eyes. She scowled at him. Luckily Jeffrey had come to the front and said to Maxim "Thank you. I feel better now. Take care of your lady. She is very good."

Maxim smiled and said "Yes, I will take care of my lady and yes, she is very good."

Alaska wanted to throw the water bottle at Maxim who was grinning at her.

Just then a man from the audience asked Alaska "Thank you for explaining so much about love, but didn't you miss something?"

He continued addressing Alaska "Normally we associate the word 'love' with romance, to marriage, to passion, to sex but you completely ignored it. Why?"

Maxim motioned Alaska to sit down and replied to the man "Because, usually marriage and sexual passion have very little to do with true love. This passion is mainly the result of hormones produced in the body and personal chemistry of the couple. Sexuality can be, and has been used as a powerful trigger to experience true divine love for thousands of years, but it is a difficult practice and it needs discipline to achieve divine connection by this process. When a romantic love is solely focused on the physical plane, it has a very short life, but if this is based on true love, the sexual union will be magical, out of this world."

Maxim continued "It is said when Eros, God of love, releases his enchanted arrow, you will feel unbridled passion and insatiable yearning for your true love for ever and ever."

Maxim stopped. There was silence in the hall.

After a short pause Maxim said "My friend, romance with your friend in the non-physical plane first, and then, see the magic of true love unfold in your life as many splendored things."

The man asked Maxim "It sounds too good to be true! Can it really be possible?"

Maxim replied "Yes, it is possible. You will get your proof if you don't get satisfied with anything less than true love in your life."

Maxim stood silently smiling at the audience. The silence stretched. No one seemed to have any desire to ask questions.

Finally he asked "No more questions?"

A woman stood up and said "Gladiator, please accept my heartfelt thanks for transforming my perception of life. I usually don't ask questions because I feel I learn more by keeping silent. But, today if you have time, could you tell us something about peace, especially on world peace? Is it possible to have world peace?"

Maxim replied "Yes, of course you can have world peace. You have the freedom to choose and create a life you want to live. I think following conditions would be conducive to world peace – you must desire/dream for a peaceful world and be passionate about it. You must be aware that the natural state of our planet is peaceful and you must have peace within yourself before you can have world peace. The last and the most important- you must be aware of your own unimaginable power and know who you truly are."

The next question came from a young man. He asked "What do you mean by saying 'you must have peace within yourself'?"

Maxim replied "I mean exactly that. You see, very few people are at peace within themselves. The greatest of battles is fought within you. Pay attention my friend. You will find variety of conflicts raging within your heart. A part of you that is called your subconscious mind, wants to keep you safe, in your comfort zone and so, it resists change. It prefers to keep you in a safe-mode. You keep doing same things day-in day-out, all safe, and so, you don't make any progress. Have you heard 'Known devil is better than the unknown'? Well, your subconscious makes you practice it and you continue living a constricted life without ever reaching your true potential."

Maxim paused for a second and then continued "There is another part of you that dreams, dreams of achieving great things. I call it the dreamer. The dreamer is passionate about its dreams.

It tries to push past the barrier erected by your subconscious mind. The dreamer is in progressive mode."

Maxim looked at the man who had asked the question and continued "Now, my friend, the stage is set for the battle to rage within you. What would you choose?-a jaded life in the safe mode or an exciting life in the progressive mode? It must be obvious to you that you evolve and progress most in the progressive mode."

The man asked "So, how can we have peace between these two modes?"

Maxim smiled and said "Know your power! Once you are aware of your immense power you easily bring a balance between the warring modes. Your limiting beliefs, regarding your own power, drop away from your subconscious mind and, the dreamer accepts reasonable safety precautions of your subconscious mind. Now, there is no conflict between the two. In other words you can say, you brought coherence between your head and heart, or your mind and body, and thus, you achieved reasonable inner peace."

Maxim paused and looked around the silent audience. He said with his usual smile "So, to have world peace, begin with yourself. Be peaceful within, and soon your dream of a peaceful world will be a reality. Peace, harmony and love will reign supreme on this beautiful planet. My ultimate magicians, you can do it."

A lady got up and said "Can I ask you one question please?"

Maxim said "Sure. Please go ahead."

She said "Could you please tell me your core message for the world? You are fond of saying you are not a spiritual teacher. The spiritual knowledge that you impart are not your teachings. Then what are you talking about? What can I take away from your seminars? What is your message, if any, for me?"

Maxim smiled and replied "You are the ultimate magician! You are god! You are the Creator– that is, my message! I am holding the door open for you. Come on in, and connect with something greater than you (the 'you' you think you are)!"

There was silence for few moments. Then a man got up and asked "What does it mean, Gladiator, in our daily lives?"

Maxim replied with his usual smile "If you can make yourself believe this truth, your life will change in miraculous ways. The moment you get the fact that indeed you are the ultimate magician who is creating this beautiful world, all your insecurities, your limitations, your doubts will drop away from you for good! You will be empowered! You will have a reason to get up in the morning, a raison d'etre, as the French call it. You are not here to struggle, my friends, but to experience and expand!"

Maxim stopped. There was silence for a few seconds, and then, as usual, the applause erupted.

CHAPTER 13

Alaska was smiling as she disconnected the phone. James had called after a gap of more than a month. He told her about everything that had happened in the period and made it sound so funny that Alaska kept laughing. After chatting with her for nearly ten minutes he said that his mother wanted to have a word with her. Alaska was surprised. She had never met her.

James's mother sounded very gentle. She said "Alaska, I have heard so much about you, I wish we could meet sometime, but just now I have a message for Gladiator. James says if I wanted my message to reach Gladiator, you were the right person for it. Please tell him I bless him, from the depth of my heart, for what he did for my son. James used to be sad, depressed, and hopeless. He had forgotten how to smile. I bless Gladiator every time I see James laugh and make others laugh with him. My son radiates joy, Alaska, and a mother's heart blesses Gladiator again and again for it, because James says it is Gladiator's magic. It is his divine power that cleared darkness from his life forever. Alaska, my child, will you tell this to Gladiator? Will you? Please?"

Alaska felt tears come to her eyes. She had quickly said "Yes. Of course I will tell him as soon as possible."

James had taken the phone and asked her "Have you met Mark recently?"

When she had said "No, not since the party", James had told her "Mark has broken off from his current girl-friend. He said it won't work."

Alaska had said "I am sorry to hear it" to which James had replied "Don't feel guilty Alaska. You are so magnetically attractive that a lot of people will fall in love with you. You possibly cannot reciprocate their feelings. Just be yourself. You will bless everyone with your un-deniable unforgettable joy and love."

Alaska had thanked him for his kind words because she did feel guilty for not loving Mark. She knew Mark was a very nice person, but now, she also knew that she had never cared for anyone in that way. She thought may be her subconscious knew someone special was meant to come in her life. Maxim was thousands of miles away in New Zealand. Alaska grumbled why he had to travel so much. He should be here, at least, for the week ends. She laughed when she heard Maxim say "Your wish is my command, Princess!" And she missed him more.

After the phone with James, Alaska, with a couple of her friends, went to cafeteria for coffee. Suddenly she felt someone was watching her. She looked up to find Jacque standing near the big window staring at her. She gave him a tentative smile but he did not respond. Her friends saw him and said "Poor Jacque! Last year he lost his girl-friend in an accident. I believe he was driving the motor-bike when they were hit by a car. He survived but she didn't. He cannot get over it."

Alaska could feel his pain. She wanted to get up and hug him, but of course she couldn't do that. She wondered when Maxim would call her. She wanted to tell him about her night-mare that had, recently, become a regular nightly feature. There was no call from Maxim, so she did her meditation and then slept.

Alaska thought she had just fallen asleep when the dreaded night-mare came. She saw the girl running towards the cliff screaming Jacque. She got up drenched in sweat. She washed her face, drank some water but could not stop crying. She didn't know why she was crying but the tears won't stop. She felt helpless. She started calling Maxim and finally fell asleep when the light of dawn was peeking from behind the curtain.

****

Alaska was walking back from her class with her friend, Meg, when her phone rang. She ignored it. She didn't want to talk with anyone today. She only wanted to talk with Maxim but looking at her watch, she knew it couldn't be him. The phone stopped ringing but the next moment it started ringing again. She let it ring. When the phone rang for the third time Meg Asked "What is wrong Alaska? Why don't you pick up the phone? May be it is your mother calling you."

"No, my mother calls on weekends only" replied Alaska sounding listless.

When the phone started ringing for the fourth time, Meg said "Let me see who is calling you" saying this she took out Alaska's phone from her bag. When she saw Maxim's photo she showed it to Alaska. Alaska grabbed the phone and excitedly said "Where are you Maxim? What is the time at your place?"

"Same as yours" said Maxim with a laugh.

"What? Where are you? Why didn't you call last night?" asked Alaska.

"Because I was on the flight and anyway, I wanted you to sleep. Now tell me exactly where you are. Ok, don't bother. I can see you." said Maxim.

"What? You are here?" asked Alaska incredulous.

"No" said Maxim.

Alaska asked "then why did you say you can see me?"

There was no answer from Maxim. Alaska said "Hello? Maxim?"

Maxim said "OK. Now turn around."

She quickly turned around and saw Maxim walking towards her. As always, she forgot the world and ran straight into his arms.

"Why you didn't tell me you were coming today?" asked Alaska.

Maxim laughed and said "As usual, I was not sure if I will be in time to catch this flight."

Maxim saw Meg standing un-certainly. He said with a smile "I am Maxim De Winter".

Meg said "Yes, I know. I am Meg. I have always wanted to meet you. I hope I can meet you when you have some free time. I have a lot of questions for Gladiator."

Alaska laughed and said "Sorry for not introducing you. Of course Meg, you will meet your Gladiator some time."

When Meg left, Maxim and Alaska crossed the road to the Lamborghini parked on the other side.

Alaska asked "Why you said 'no' when I asked if you were here?"

"So that you don't run across the road without looking left or right and give me another heart-attack." replied Maxim with a smile.

Alaska mumbled "No, I don't do that."

Maxim asked "Where do you want to go? What do you want to eat?"

Alaska replied "Where ever you want Maxim, but tell me how come you are here in the middle of the week?"

Maxim looked at her and said softly "I thought someone wanted to see me soon."

After a moment he said "I cannot let you cry Princess. It breaks my heart. Let us go to the coffee shop at the hotel. Hopefully it will not be crowded at this time and we can talk."

Maxim drove to the hotel and soon they were seated at a table near a window by an over-enthusiastic waiter. Maxim, without looking at the menu, ordered lemon iced tea and chicken sandwich with fries and said to the waiter "That will be all." The waiter showed him the wine list. Maxim stopped him "No! I don't need anything. I will call if we need coffee."

Alaska was surprised at his curtness. She looked at Maxim with a question in her eyes.

Maxim reached for her hands and said "I have travelled for nearly twenty hours to be with you. I don't want to waste time looking at the wine list."

Alaska looked concerned and asked "I hope you could sleep on the flight."

Maxim said "I can hardly relax when you are in pain, Princess! Alright, now tell me what happened."

Alaska first told him about Jacque's girlfriend dying in the road accident and Jacque not being able to get over it thinking he was responsible for her death.

The waiter got their food. They ate in silence. Alaska knew Maxim was busy with his thoughts, so she kept quiet. So, when she looked up, she was surprised to find him looking at her with intense concentration.

Maxim said "OK. Now tell me about your night-mare."

Alaska swallowed and took a sip of iced-tea before saying slowly "Maxim, now I know the girl, the girl in my night-mare who screams 'Jacque'. It is me but why I am screaming? Why I jumped of the cliff? Was Jacque there? What was happening? I find it very painful. I can hardly stop crying when I think of Jacque. Maxim, who is or was Jacque?"

Maxim gently said "I was Jacque. I was Jacque, a commoner, who had the audacity to publically announce 'I love the princess and I will carry her off', for which, of course, I was punished. And that is also the reason why I call you Princess. You were my king's daughter, the un-attainable Princess. Just before I was put to death, I had promised myself that I will come again and I will carry the princess off and this time, I will live and not die, for my princess."

Alaska's eyes were open wide in horror, as if she was watching the gruesome scene. Tears were flowing unchecked from her eyes.

Maxim gently said "It is a time for celebration, Princess, not for tears. I kept my promise to myself. You are with me and here I am living for you."

Alaska was looking blindly at him and suddenly cried "Jacque?"

Maxim nodded and said "Yes, Princess."

Alaska couldn't control herself any longer. She quickly got up from her chair to run away but Maxim caught her in his arms and hugged her close. Alaska pressed her face in his chest and tried to cover her face with the lapel of his jacket and sobbed uncontrollably. Maxim rocked her gently like a child and kept murmuring "It is OK Princess, it is OK."

Other diners sitting near their table had stopped eating and were looking at them in concern. An elderly couple came and asked "Can we be of any help?"

Maxim smiled at them but continued murmuring softly to sooth Alaska. When Alaska calmed down Maxim asked her "Better?" Alaska looked up at Maxim through tear drenched eyes and nodded her head. Maxim wiped her tears. Alaska wrapped her arms around him and laid her head gently on his chest.

The lady still standing near them, asked again "Can we be of any help?"

Her companion said "May be not. I think the lady already has in her arms what her heart desires."

Alaska smiled mistily at him and said "Yes. Thank you."

After a little while Maxim asked "Coffee?"

Alaska nodded and said "Yes, but first I need to blow my nose and wash my face. But, at the same time, I don't want to leave Jacque!"

Maxim smiled and said "That is easily solved. I will accompany you. Hopefully there won't be any woman to scream 'murder' on the sight of your Jacque."

Alaska giggled and said "Get the coffee. I will be back in a jiffy."

When they were having coffee, Alaska asked "Love does transcend physical death. Doesn't it Jacque?"

Maxim gently said "Yes. Love does. Are you going to call me 'Jacque' now?"

Alaska said "Oh, did I say Jacque? I was thinking about him. He was so much fun- always made me laugh, daring the palace guards to catch him, easily jumping over high walls, and oh, he had such beautiful Indigo eyes! Is that why, Maxim, your Indigo eyes fascinate me? Whenever you look at me or I look into your eyes I shift to another dimension, a dimension where I feel cherished beyond words!"

Maxim picked up Alaska's hands and said "You are cherished literally beyond words my Princess!"

Alaska didn't say a word. She held tightly to Maxim's hands and dreamily kept looking into his Indigo eyes.

When Maxim saw Alaska rubbing her eyes, he said "Time for bed, Little-one. Your eyes are swollen with all that crying and lack of sleep." Saying this, he guided Alaska to the Lamborghini.

CHAPTER 14

Alaska was happy. A sense of well-being was bubbling inside her. She couldn't stop smiling. Maxim had totally surprised her. A minute ago he had called to say he was on way to pick her up for dinner. She quickly got dressed and ran out to wait for Maxim, but the Indigo Lamborghini was already there, waiting for her! She got in the car and said "Hi Maxim! Aren't you early?"

"Hi Princess! May be the Lamborghini knows how impatient I am to see you." murmured Maxim.

Alaska smiled and said "You say such nice things Maxim! But how come you could come here again on a week day?"

Maxim replied "I guess, one of the privileges of being the boss! Anyway, this weekend I won't be able to come. I will be thousands of miles away. OK, where do you want to have dinner?"

"Anywhere will do, where we can talk. I have to tell you a lot of things." Alaska said excitedly.

Maxim drove to his hotel and took her to the coffee shop. He met an acquaintance on way to the coffee shop. As Alaska made to move on, Maxim caught her hand and made the introductions and said "My friend, Alaska." Same thing he did again when he met a couple in the coffee shop. Alaska wanted to laugh at the expression on their faces when Maxim said 'my friend, Alaska'.

Finally, when they were seated and had placed their orders, Alaska asked "Maxim, why did you introduce me to your friends as 'my friend'?"

Maxim smiled and said "Aren't you my friend? Anyway the people we met just now are not my friends. They are acquaintances."

Alaska said "Oh, you should have seen the look they gave me when you said I was your friend, as if I was an interloper trying to enter the hallowed world of the rich and famous."

Maxim laughed and said "No, they looked at you like that because I have never introduced a lady, as my friend."

Alaska asked curiously "Really? Then why did you introduce me as one?"

Maxim softly said "Because you are one! Simple, my dear Watson!"

Alaska smiled but said nothing. Maxim looked deeply in her beautiful eyes and said "I am going to hold the next board meeting of De Winter Enterprises here in Boston. I want you to attend it. You will learn how things are done in corporate world in general and in particular, how De Winter Enterprises make its billions."

Alaska looked surprised. She had no idea how business was done, let alone making billion dollars.

Maxim could read her thoughts and said "You will learn to make billions, if you wanted to do so, but, this time, I want you to be present mainly to help me. Yes, Princess, it would be great to have a friend give me new ideas to improve the running of De Winter Enterprises."

Alaska was so surprised that, without thinking, she blurted out "I? I help you in running your business? I know nothing about it. Sorry Maxim, I won't be able to assist you in this."

Maxim looked at Alaska with an unfathomable expression in his Indigo eyes for a long moment.

He said slowly emphasizing each word "If I wanted an assistant, I could have a dozen in a minute, an assistant who walks a step behind me with a note pad in his hands, ever ready to do my bidding and hoping to get my approval."

Maxim stopped for a second, and then continued "No, Princess, you got it all wrong if you thought I was looking for someone to assist me and always follow me like a puppy. I want you, Princess, to walk with me, challenge me, correct me and teach me! Get out of the habit of believing you are 'less than' I am or anyone else for that matter. You are not! You cannot be, Princess! You are boundless Awareness beyond time and space with total freedom to be, to do and to have anything you choose to be!"

Maxim stopped and looked at Alaska with a gentle smile and said "Princess, my little magician, I dreamed of you working with me, playing with me, having fun together and taking millions along with us for a joy ride of their life time, shining light on them to show it is possible to live a life beyond their wildest dreams."

After a little pause Maxim asked "Will you play with me Princess?"

Alaska had tears in her eyes. With a gentle smile she replied "Yes, Maxim, I will play with you."

Soon, their food arrived. As usual, they shared every experience they could think of. Alaska told Maxim about meeting Jacque.

She said "I met him last week at the cafeteria. He still feels guilty about his friend's death. Could you talk to him sometime Maxim? He helped me remember my 'Jacque', so I want to help him."

Maxim said "Sure, I will, whenever we can meet him."

After a little pause Maxim said "Could you give me your parents' telephone number? I want to invite them for dinner that evening at the multi-cuisine restaurant at the hotel. I believe they are having something special that Saturday.

Alaska groaned.

Maxim laughed and said "Still resisting, are you? OK, you don't have to come, if you don't want to. I will meet them and later take them for the dinner. Can I have the number?"

Alaska said "I will call them later and tell them."

Maxim reached for her hand and said with a teasing smile "Evading? Don't look so crest-fallen. I know what they will ask me and I assure you my answer will satisfy them. Let us call them now. Don't you trust your Jacque?"

With great reluctance, Alaska telephoned her parents and Maxim spoke with both her parents and made the evening arrangements to their satisfaction.

After a short silence Maxim gently lifted Alaska's chin a little and kept looking at her, but Alaska wouldn't meet his eyes.

Maxim murmured softly "Won't you speak, Princess?"

Alaska mumbled "Nothing to talk."

Maxim smiled and said "I thought someone had lots to tell me. Well, then, let me tell you what I had to tell you."

He said "The next seminar we are going to attend is in Rhinebeck. It is on Saturday, the 7th. We have been invited by a group in their early twenty who are keen to learn some spiritual truths to live a better and more successful life."

"Really? When do we go?" asked Alaska all excited.

Maxim laughed and replied "We can go on 7th morning and return on 8th. I can treat you to a grand dinner on 7th. Would you like that?"

Alaska forgot her earlier annoyance and said "Yes! Where shall we go?"

Maxim said "I will check the restaurants in the neighborhood and let you know. You can choose. Are you ready for some dessert and coffee?"

When they had finished with their dessert, Maxim softly reminded Alaska "Princess, this seminar at Rhinebeck is going to be slightly different from others. Remember, you will be presenting it and I will be sitting with the audience."

Alaska said "Oh" and remained silent.

Maxim smiled and tucked her hair behind her ears, as he always did, in a gentle caressing way and said "This seminar is going to be an extra-ordinary one. Do you know why Princess? I know you are not aware of it, but you simply radiate a combination of love and joy where ever you go. You uplift their vibration. The audience will fall in love with you without even knowing why. No need to worry about it. You are there because they need you. They need your help.

Your only goal is, to first sense their needs and second, to help them as best as you can."

Maxim stopped but kept looking at Alaska with his gentle understanding smile. After a moment Alaska asked "Will I really be able to help them Maxim?"

Maxim replied "Absolutely! Again, you are not aware of your own spiritual knowledge and that is why you doubt. There cannot be a question to which you don't have an answer!"

Maxim continued "Dorothy will work out the best way to reach Rhinebeck and let us know our travel plans. You know, Mark, Brian and your parents want to attend your first seminar. Do you want them to come?"

Alaska said "My parents would be very disappointed if we don't tell them. I will call them tonight."

Maxim nodded and asked "Am I pushing you too much? You see, Princess, when you choose to come into 3D world, you are bound by the physical limitations of time and space. The clock of the linear time is ticking away. You have only so much time to usher in an era of love and harmony on this planet. I know you will achieve all this in the time you have allotted yourself for the purpose. Smile my friend. You can do it and you will do it!"

Alaska said "Maxim, sometimes you overwhelm me. You remind me that this creation, which appears so solid, is just a game that we are playing in our boundless awareness. It is not the real reality, so to speak. It is a kind of virtual reality we are creating to have varied experiences and thus, keep expanding, and so, no use getting attached to one!"

Maxim, who was holding her hands, said to Alaska "Yes, that is the truth. Do you want some more coffee or shall we go?"

Alaska declined coffee and asked Maxim "When do I see you?"

Maxim replied "You tell me when you want to see me. Princess, you always say 'soon', which means you leave it to me to choose when I come. Give me a date, a time and see me obey your command! You have never used the power bestowed upon you by your Jacque."

Alaska was astonished to hear it. She asked "You mean you will come whenever I ask you to come?"

Maxim guided her to the Lamborghini and said with a smile "Try it sometime!"

CHAPTER 15

Alaska's parents were thrilled to know about the seminar she was going to present in Rhinebeck. Her parents had decided to join her in New York on her arrival from Boston and then to drive with Maxim and Alaska to Rhinebeck. But, just a few minutes ago her father had called and said that they will not be able to come after all because her mother was down with some kind of viral fever. She had very high temperature and the doctors were doing all kinds of tests to find the cause for the fever. He had asked Alaska to send a video recording of the seminar. Alaska's mother was very disappointed. Alaska herself was also feeling disappointed. She looked at the watch and called Maxim to inform him about her mother, hoping he would not be busy with one of his meetings.

Maxim picked up the phone and said "What a pleasant surprise Princess!"

Alaska quickly asked "Are you busy? Are you alone?"

Maxim laughed and replied "Not exactly alone, but I am sure Brian and Dorothy will excuse me for five minutes."

"Well, Maxim, my mom is sick and she cannot come for the seminar." said Alaska.

Maxim said "That is sad. I was looking forward to meeting them."

Alaska asked "Why? You are going to meet them soon. Aren't you?"

"Yes, Princess, but I want to know them better and the easiest way to do that is to meet often."

Alaska said "Well, I suppose so. Anyway they are really looking forward to your visit and the dinner."

Maxim softly asked "You will be coming for the dinner, won't you Princess?"

Alaska asked "Will it make any difference?"

Maxim thought for a moment and said "Hmmm, let us see. For Jacque, a day without you would have been like a day without the life giving Sun!"

Alaska said "Really? And what about you Maxim?"

Maxim said "It would be like a sail-boat without the wind behind it, dancing without the music, playing piano with no sound, and serenading Princess, with no Princess around!"

Alaska laughed and said "How can you think and say such things with Brian and Dorothy listening?"

Maxim laughed and replied "Well, you will have to ask them how they tolerate my literary rhetoric on a working afternoon. Alright let me get back to my work. See you soon and in the meantime, smile and enchant the world as always!"

Alaska said "So long, see you soon." She wondered how Maxim could be so poetic and so much fun in this physical reality while remaining aware of his non-physical True-self.

****

Maxim was on way to Alaska's dorm to take her to the airport for their morning flight to New York. Alaska was ready with her little suitcase when Mr. Mendoza stopped the car. He jumped out to take her suitcase saying a cheery 'good morning madam' with a broad smile. Maxim got out from the back seat. He looked at Alaska and said "Good morning, Princess, you do make the morning wonderful. Let us go."

Soon they were all checked-in and sitting with coffee at the airport waiting to board the flight.

Maxim asked "Did you sleep well?"

Alaska moaned "How could I? I know, you don't want me to say it, but it would have been great if you were presenting and I was sitting with the audience. And Mom sent a new dress for me to wear at the presentation and that made me feel more nervous!"

Maxim laughed and said "Forget it, Princess. Tell me about your research. Your friends! Your Jacque!"

Alaska asked "Which Jacque you are talking about? My Jacque or the French guy in my class?"

Maxim asked "My Jacque? Do you still have those night-mares?"

Alaska replied "No, I don't have night-mares anymore, but, I do dream about him, quite often. He was so much fun to be with! It is confusing but sometimes I do sense his presence and feel him laughing and teasing me. He feels so real, Maxim, I feel I can touch him. I wonder how or why I feel like that."

Maxim looked intently at her for a short while before replying "Yes, I was your Jacque, in the past life, but in the quantum field there is no limitation of time or space. That means, everything is happening in the eternal now, at the same time, so to speak. So, if you focus more on or feel attracted to Jacque, you will shift to that dimension and feel that to be 'real'. I had some difficult experiences myself. Several times I had tough time controlling a strong urge to pick you up, Princess, in my arms, as Jacque used to do. I knew you, Alaska, may not be able to appreciate my behavior, so I had to crush Jacque's desire that still lives through me."

Maxim stopped. Maxim and Alaska sat there looking at each other with a deep an unexplainable emotion, an emotion that had transcended the physical death of Jacque and Princess, centuries ago.

They sat there gazing at each other, dead to the hustle-bustle of the airport. Suddenly, Maxim heard the last call for their flight to New York. He got up and said with a laugh "Come on Princess, we are the last ones to board the flight."

It was a short flight to New York. As soon as they landed there, they headed for a restaurant to have a hearty breakfast before driving to Rhinebeck. They were busy with their food when a lady came and hesitatingly asked "Are you Gladiator?"

Maxim replied with his usual smile "Some people prefer to call me Gladiator."

The lady said "I know this is not the time or the place but could you please answer just one question for me? I have been trying to attend your seminars but somehow I always miss them. Today, when I saw you at the airport, I followed you to the restaurant."

Maxim, without replying, looked at her for a long moment and said "Yes, I have powers, powers, that people think are special to me. I own them because they are part of my true essence, and I want to inform you that you too have the same powers! You have remained imprisoned in your mind believing in human imperfections and powerlessness! Change your belief which will change your perception of the world and which will transform you!"

There was silence for a moment. The lady looked absolutely drum-struck by the reply. She said "Oh my God, oh my God, how did you know what I was going to ask you?"

Maxim replied with a smile "Never mind how I knew your question. You got the answer. If you will excuse us we are in a hurry to drive to Rhinebeck after our breakfast."

The lady said "Oh, yes, yes. Sorry." and left them to have their breakfast in peace.

Alaska asked Maxim "Weren't you a bit curt with the lady?"

Maxim replied "I could see she was all set to sit with us for an hour or so. I have other plans. I want to be with you and besides, we should be leaving for Rhinebeck soon."

While driving to Rhinebeck they discussed everything on Earth except the evening seminar. Alaska was trying to forget but was not succeeding.

Finally Maxim said with a smile "Relax Princess! This evening seminar is going to be great. I have seen the preview. Believe me!"

Alaska nodded her head, but didn't say a word.

Maxim asked "Do you remember the witch from the island?"

Alaska replied "Yes. What about her?"

Maxim said "She wants to meet us. She has sent a message. It says 'now is the time for celebration'."

Alaska asked "Celebration? What does she mean? Celebrate what?"

Maxim said "You will find out when you meet her."

Alaska asked "Where is she? How can I meet her?"

Maxim replied "She is already in L.A. After your Masters, when you join the spiritual school in L.A., you will meet her. Princess, you want to come to L.A., don't you?"

Alaska's eyes shone with excitement. She said "Yes, yes, Maxim, yes. I told my parents."

Maxim laughed and asked her "Do you want to know the so called, purpose of your life?"

Alaska asked "Yes. What is it?"

Maxim replied "You are going to be a Fashionista, a world famous Fashionista, who will change the present trend of fashion!"

Alaska looked deflated and said "What? Fashion? I know nothing about fashion and I don't particularly care about it."

Maxim replied "A Fashionista! Check the dictionary. Princess, mark my words. You will usher-in an era of a new fashion, not in haute couture, not in clothes, but in something else. What is that something else? You will have to find out. Are you curious to know what your heart truly desires and dreams?"

Involuntarily the thought arose in her mind "You Maxim!"

She got the silent answer in her mind "You already have him."

Alaska quickly looked at Maxim. His eyes were fixed straight ahead on the road. She could spy a little smile on his lips, but, as he didn't say anything, Alaska kept quiet.

After a short silence Alaska asked "Tell me, Maxim, the purpose of your life. You say you not a spiritual teacher, then what are you- an entrepreneur par excellence, a successful wizard, a fashion model, a handsome lady-killer, a charmer, a hypnotist, a wise scholar or what?"

Maxim remained silent for some time and then, said "You will know when the time is right, Princess!"

After a short silence they carried on sharing news till they reached the resort in Rhinebeck. On their arrival, they were received by the host for the evening seminar. Maxim had already informed her that Alaska would be presenting the seminar although he would be present to answer questions. The host, a lady, looked at Alaska from her head to toe in disbelief.

She asked "Isn't she too young to present a seminar on spirituality?"

Maxim replied with a smile "Spirituality is the study of spirit, of who we truly are. We are non-physical, multidimensional beings, beyond time and space. So, the linear age of the lady can have no effect on her spiritual knowledge, what so ever! Don't you agree with me?"

Maxim's smile coupled with his quizzing look completely flustered the lady. She quickly said "Yes. Yes, of course." and left them.

After checking-in in the resort, Maxim and Alaska went to find something to eat at the coffee shop. That was a mistake they soon realized. The place was buzzing with hundreds of over-enthusiastic young audience. Questions kept pouring at them. Finally Maxim said with a laugh "Give us time to have some sustenance, otherwise, by the evening we won't have the strength to answer your questions."

The barrage of questions reduced but most of them hung around them.

Maxim murmured "Look at your plate and eat, and please do not dazzle them with your smile."

Alaska smiled but kept looking at her plate. After their meal they went back to their rooms. They had planned to check out the auditorium but thought not to do so to avoid the enthusiastic crowd still following them.

Alone in her room, Alaska took out her new dress that Mom had sent for her first presentation. It looked like a Japanese Kimono with beautiful embroidery and a wide belt at the waist that totally covered her solar plexus. She looked in the mirror and debated what to do with her hair- pile up or leave it flowing. She kept herself busy thinking of things of no consequence to avoid worrying about the evening presentation. Maxim had said "trust me" and that is what she was going to do.

The seminar was at 5 PM. Alaska decided to take a shower now and then dress at her leisure. She telephoned her parents. Her mother was feeling better but the doctors were still awaiting the Lab results.

Her mother said 'Aly, my child, we are thrilled. We are so proud of you. I could never have imagined that one day you would be teaching spirituality to the world, that you would bring joy to so many people by your talks."

Alaska said "Mom, I need your blessings."

Her mother said "You have our blessings. I wonder if you know what you mean to us Aly!"

As Alaska finished her talk with her parents, her phone rang. It was Maxim.

He asked "How is your mother?"

Alaska replied "Mother is disappointed but she is better."

Maxim said "We will take her for your next presentation. Princess, we will leave at 4.45 PM so that we have enough time to check the auditorium."

After a short pause Maxim said "Princess?"

Alaska said "What?"

Maxim said softly "Won't you smile for me?"

Alaska smiled and heard Maxim say "Beautiful! See you soon."

She got ready and came out of her room at 4.45 and as always, Maxim looking debonair, was waiting for her.

Maxim looked into her eyes and said "stunningly beautiful, aren't you Princess?"

Alaska smiled and curtsied to him saying "Thank you kind sir. I must say you yourself look irresistibly attractive. Watch out for all the damsels falling in love with you tonight!"

Maxim took her hands and asked "What about this damsel? Will she fall in love with me tonight?"

Alaska looked at Maxim in confusion. Maxim smiled and said "let us go."

Soon they reached the auditorium and the host was there to welcome them. She took them to the side door which directly opened on to the stage. Maxim checked the lights and the sound system and then came back to Alaska where he had asked her to wait for him. He took her hands in his and looked long and deep in her eyes. The host came to ask him to come to the stage and be introduced. Maxim again asked Alaska to wait for him and went to the stage with the host. After the formal introduction, the host left him standing alone under the spot light.

Maxim smiled and waved to the audience and announced "My ultimate magicians, allow me to present Alaska, your magical guide for the evening" saying this he pulled Alaska in the center of the round spot light and walked away from the stage.

For a moment there was hushed silence in the hall. She looked dainty, delicate and beautiful. Was she real? She stood alone. The young audience waited with abated breath for her to speak. Alaska closed her eyes for a second to ascertain the vibration of her audience, but when she opened her eyes she was shocked to see the hall packed and more. It seemed to her that thousand pairs of eyes were glued on her. She forgot that she was here to help them live happier lives. Her mind went blank and she remained still like a statue. Just then she saw something move on the upper floor. She looked up and saw Maxim laughing and waving both of his hands at her. She smiled and waved back. He blew a flying kiss and she laughed out loud and returned the kiss.

There was an appreciative roar from the audience, who, probably thought, the kiss was for them. Alaska, still laughing, looked at the young audience and said "Hey, you, Gladiator's ultimate magicians, what dream are you dreaming into existence this evening? Whatever it may be, I am all the way with you!"

And again there was an appreciative roar from the audience..........

To be continued...........

ABOUT THE AUTHOR

Alcyoné Sumila Starr, a science graduate, loves Astronomy, Quantum physics, spiritual studies and all things esoteric. After decades of research and meditation, she writes to demystify basic universal laws to bring hope, harmony and happiness to all humanity in the most natural and effortless way. Her mission is to inspire, awaken and acquaint millions to their own inherent power to create and to live the life of their dreams.

She has participated in an international conference held in Brasilia, Brazil. She had presented a paper titled "Civilian Capacity Building: The spiritual Dimension", which was published as an annexure in the book titled "Civilian Capacity Building for Peace Operations in a Changing World Order" in 2013.

She has written articles mainly on spirituality. Her article "Building Bridges: A spiritual Approach" was published by Fair Observer – http://www.fairobserver.com/culture/building-bridges-spiritual-approach/.

She welcomes questions from her readers. She can be reached by email at shikamesh@gmail.com and on her Facebook page.